The Ghost in Allie's Pool

Sari Bodi

Brown Barn Books
Weston, Connecticut

Brown Barn Books
A division of Pictures of Record, Inc.
119 Kettle Creek Road, Weston, Connecticut 06883, U.S.A.

The Ghost in Allie's Pool
Copyright © 2007, by Sari Bodi

Library of Congress Cataloging-in-Publication Data

Bodi, Sari, 1954–
  The ghost in Allie's pool / Sari Bodi.
    p. cm.
  Summary: Eighth-grader Allie Toth is visited by a ghost who committed suicide during the voyage of the Mayflower, while at the same time her best friend Marissa has dropped her for a more popular crowd, whose members definitely do not like Allie. Includes facts about Dorothy May Bradford and other Mayflower passengers.
  ISBN 978-0-9768126-6-1 (alk. paper)
[1. Ghosts—Fiction. 2. Bullies—Fiction. 3. Friendship—Fiction. 4. Popularity—Fiction. 5. Mayflower (Ship)—Fiction. 6. Schools—Fiction.] I. Title.

  PZ7.B63524Gh 2007
  [Fic]—dc22

      2006039743

For my parents,
whose love of family history
taught me that where we come from
is an important part
of who we are.

ACKNOWLEDGEMENTS

Since in many ways this book is about family history, I would like to acknowledge my families—both past and present.

First of all, many thanks to my mother, Sara Lord Bodi, who discovered the story of Dorothy May while tracing our roots back to twelve passengers on the Mayflower. And to my father, Lewis J. Bodi, whose tales of growing up in a Hungarian immigrant household inspired me to tell stories myself. Those sharing my branch of the family tree—Betsy, Nancy, and Kip—will always treasure our parents' stories of their pasts.

I am grateful to my husband, Eric Montgomery, and our children, Ming and Luke, for enthusiastically supporting my writing. And for not complaining too much about all the take-out dinners.

Then there are the other kinds of families we form. The members of my children's book writing group, who have combed through every word of my manuscript with creativity, good humor, and café lattes—Michaela MacColl, Christine Pakkala, and Karen Swanson. Also, Cameron Stracher, who explained legal terms using words I could actually understand.

And to my other writing companions who've supplied me with excellent advice and—when feeling ambitious—home-made cookies—Jane Burns, Lisa Clair, Linda Howard, Russ Miller, Ray Rauth, Caroline Rosenstone, and Pat Thornton.

Thanks to Patricia Reilly Giff, an extraordinary teacher, who created a family of children's book writers at The Dinosaur's Paw.

Also, Nancy Hammerslough, publisher of Brown Barn Books, who took a chance on a first-time novelist to help me create a family of readers.

And finally, I'd like to remember my English and Hungarian ancestors whose distant lives I've often imagined.

1

If Dorothy May hadn't jumped off the Mayflower on a freezing cold Cape Cod night in 1620, I wouldn't have been born. So shouldn't I be happier with my life?

I'm sitting on the curb in front of Bristol Pizza with my best friend Marissa, waiting for the cool kids to show up. Marissa says we need to be more popular before we get to high school. I don't see why; we have each other.

I really shouldn't be here. My paper on "digging up the roots of your family tree" is due in Mr. Sampson's English class tomorrow. Mr. Sampson says it's important for us to know who we are by where we came from. "And I don't just mean writing down the name of your parents," he said. "You already did that in kindergarten."

"Hey, Allie. Do what I'm going to do," Marissa says, slurping the last of her diet soda through a straw. "Tell Mr. Sampson your mother had a nervous breakdown and you had to go to the hospital with her."

"Yeah, that would really work since she's the school psychologist," I say, chewing on the warm crust of my second piece of sausage pizza.

"Why not? Tell him your mom couldn't deal with the kids anymore so she went crazy." Marissa smiles at me like she just came up with the greatest idea.

I'm not in the mood for smiling. We've been waiting for over an hour on this hard curb and my stomach is killing me from wearing the tight jeans Marissa lent me so the cool kids won't think I'm a nerd. According to her, we already have a couple of strikes against us because we're in the smart eighth-grade class.

Marissa tucks the clinging pink shirt her mother just bought her into her low-cut skirt and looks over her shoulder to admire herself in the pizza-place window. "Do I look fat?" she asks.

"Right." I roll my eyes. Marissa has the tiniest waist. But then, she has the tiniest everything—the tiniest nose, the tiniest feet. Next to her, I look like King Kong. I'm only thirteen and I already have a size 9½ shoe.

"We really should go to the library." I open the genealogical chart my mother gave me. There are black lines connecting my name to my mother's and father's, my mother's line eventually branching off to England, my father's to Hungary. My mother spends every spare moment finding genealogical websites on the Internet, tracking her ancestors—all people connected to me by blood, but who I'll never know.

If I drew a chart of all the friends I've had over the years, all the black lines would connect them to Marissa. She's the friendly one. I'm shy. Ever since I first met her in kindergarten, Marissa would walk up to anyone and say, "Wanna play with us?" And before you knew it, she'd organize a gang of kids to play four-square, secret spy games, or collect jars full of odd-looking bugs.

"I'm glad my mother's not obsessed with her dead relatives." Marissa pulls back the sleeve of her pink cardigan to look at her watch and I notice she's not wearing the bracelet I gave her with a fairy charm dangling from it. Engraved on a disk attached to the charm are the initials "M&A, BFF," which means "Marissa and Allie, Best Friends Forever." I'm wearing mine around my neck on a silver chain.

"You're lucky," I say. "Your mother isn't always telling you how proud you should be that you're descended from someone who came over on the Mayflower."

"Doesn't she know how uncool it is to be descended from anyone as totally white as the Pilgrims?" She draws a line of diet soda on the pavement with her straw.

I shrug. I wish I was descended from a mother like Marissa's who used to model for *Vogue* magazine so I could have inherited beautiful straight blonde hair and a small Irish nose. Mom says someday I'll be happy to have the so-called porcelain skin I inherited from my English ancestors. But right now I look like a ghost next to Marissa, whose mother lets her go to a tanning salon to get a spray-on tan.

Suddenly Marissa hisses. "Here come Crystal and Suzanne. Fix your hair. It's doing that frizzy thing."

"I can't help it. It is frizzy."

Marissa frantically grabs a brush out of her bag and jabs it at my head trying to get my wiry red hair to behave, but it doesn't matter how much she brushes, it still sticks up all over my head like porcupine quills. She gives up and ties an elastic band around it, then whispers, "Pretend we're having an interesting conversation." She sneaks a look at Crystal and Suzanne walking towards us, swinging their hips and flipping their long straight hair as if they expect all eyes to be on them. They're a salt-and-pepper pair—Crystal's white-blonde hair streaming down her back contrasting with Suzanne's dark ponytail.

"Okay." I glance at the name Dorothy May on the chart. "My mother told me this story about one of my ancestors whose wife jumped off the Mayflower and killed herself."

"Do me a favor," Marissa cuts me off. "Don't bore Crystal and Suzanne with that stuff." To Marissa, ancient history is an Instant Message that came five seconds ago, so something that happened four hundred years ago is beyond boring.

Before the girls reach us, Marissa rushes to them and gives them big hugs, leaving me on the curb. Everyone in the parking lot is probably staring at me, whispering, "There's that girl with the pale skin, frizzy red hair, and no friends." I start breathing really fast. I wish I was at the library working on my family-tree paper like I'm supposed to be.

Everything was fine this summer. When we weren't practicing cheerleading routines Marissa had learned from her cousin, we lazed around on rafts in my pool talking till nighttime. But right before school started, Marissa decided she wanted to go to the public pool to track down the popular girls so she could get into their clique. These girls were the pretty ones who always seem to be having more fun than anyone else.

And that's when she started hanging out with Crystal and Suzanne. They're beautiful and great lacrosse players. They're also kind of mean. In our school, you can't get any cooler than that.

Finally, Marissa walks back over to me. She's smiling kind of funny.

"They want me to come with them to Crystal's house. Crystal's mother's not home, and some boys are going to meet us there." She takes lip-gloss out of her pocketbook and rolls it across her lips. They shine in the sun.

I stand up and stretch out my stiff legs. "Okay, how far is it? Can we walk?"

She looks at the ground. "Uh, they didn't say anything about you coming, and I'd ask them, I really would, but I don't know them well enough."

I feel like I'm going to throw up sausage pizza. "What about your mother?" My voice sounds stupid and husky as if I'm going to cry. "She's supposed to pick us up."

"Sorry," says Marissa. "I have to go. They're waiting." And she points to Crystal and Suzanne, who are starting to walk away. "I'll call you later."

I watch Marissa leave me, her skirt slung low, her shoulders still tan from summer, and her blonde hair bouncing. She must have washed it three times while I was waiting for her this morning.

A tear rolls down my face. "Don't be such a wimpy-doodle," I yell at myself, using the word Marissa and I made up for cry-baby. But another tear follows the first one as I think of the long walk home by myself.

As I reach for the genealogical chart my mother gave me, I accidentally knock it into a muddy puddle. I quickly pick it up, noticing that the name Dorothy May is now smudged.

I wonder if Dorothy May felt as lonely as I do on the night she jumped off the Mayflower. She spent two months crossing the Atlantic Ocean on a tiny, crowded ship with a man who didn't love her. The most depressing part is that after Dorothy killed herself, her husband married the woman he truly loved. And that woman and Dorothy's husband are my ancestors.

I suppose I should be grateful that because Dorothy May sacrificed her life, I'm alive. But right now I'm not too happy with the life I have.

2

When I get home, I try to sneak past my brother who's playing on his computer in the family room, which is stuffed with antique furniture handed down to my mother by her relatives. My father says it looks like there's a tag sale going on in here, and threatens to put price tags on everything.

"Hey, Smelly Allie, Mom's looking for you," Will shouts out.

I grab a handful of his potato chips and stuff them into my mouth. "I'm telling Mom you're eating at the computer."

He doesn't look up from his game. His long, skinny fingers tap wildly on the keyboard as he kills a couple hundred terrorists. Will thinks he's so great because he's a sophomore in high school. Marissa says he could be a rock star with his thick, wavy blonde hair. I think he's disgusting.

"Don't touch my chips. I don't want to have to detox them, Smelly Allie." My brother gave me that nickname because one time, when I was walking our dog, I stepped in his poop.

"Stop calling me that, you big turd. Your stupid friend Alex yelled it out of his car window yesterday."

Will laughs. "Well, Smelly Allie, that should be an incentive to take more baths."

"If I start calling you Stupid Will, does that mean you'll start passing your math tests?" I practically spit this at him.

His fingers stall for a moment and he stares at me with his blue-green eyes. I got stuck with the muddy-brown ones. "You wait until you take algebra instead of that baby math you take now."

"Whatever you say, Stupid Will."

"SMELLY ALLIE!"

⧗

My mother's working in her bedroom and I don't want to have to lie to her about going to the library, so I hold my breath when I walk past her room. On the wall near her door, I notice a framed picture I drew of Mom and me when I was five years old. I drew myself with a toothy smile and curly red hair flying out of my head. I drew my mother's lips like a heart.

Whenever my mother looks at this picture, she says, "Someday you'll love me like that again." I do love my mother, but she can be pretty embarrassing.

"Allie, come here!" she calls out. "I found something you might be able to use for your family-tree paper."

I'm caught. As I stand in her doorway, I see Mom at her antique desk surfing the genealogy websites on her laptop. I guess there was someone like Mom in every generation to make sure all the family history got handed down to the next generation. I hope she doesn't expect me to be that person.

"Where's Marissa?" my mother asks, pushing her tortoise-shell glasses up on her nose. "I thought she was coming over for dinner."

"She wanted to finish her paper at home." I try not to look at my mother.

"That's okay. More frozen macaroni and cheese for us," my mother says. As usual, her hair's a mess—the grey is showing through the brown. She always waits until the last minute to go to the salon. She's wearing the sloppy at-home clothes she puts on every day after work—navy-blue sweat-pants and a sweatshirt.

"Mom, did anyone tell you sweatsuits are for old people in nursing homes?"

"Oh, good. When it's my time to go, I'll fit right in." She waves me over to her desk. "Look at this." She points to the image on her computer screen of a fancy house. "This was the manor house of your ancestor, Alice Carpenter, when she was married to her first husband. Maybe we can take a trip to England and visit it next summer."

"Why would I want to go to a boring old house? We haven't even been to Disney World."

"I've told you, Disney World is for people with no imagi-nations. They have to have everything created for them. It is a small world, after all." She hits "print" and twelve copies of Alice's house print out. She'll place these in binders labeled "Our Pilgrim Ancestors" and send them to all our relatives. I can't imagine any of them actually reading it; no one in the family is as obsessed with our ancestry as Mom is.

"Why can't you just be a normal mother?" I ask.

"I thought you might be interested in seeing the house of the woman you were named after."

"She has nothing to do with me." I wish she'd stop trying to teach me things all the time. It's not like I don't get enough education in school where I spend most of my life.

"She has something to do with you. There's a tiny piece of her DNA floating around inside you." She draws a circle on my stomach.

"Do I look like her?"

"There aren't any pictures of her, but I've always imagined that she had curly red hair like yours."

"I'll bet her mother wouldn't let her dye it blonde either." I pull the elastic band off my ponytail so my hair falls around my shoulders in a big clumpy mess. I glance at myself in the mirror over my great-grandmother's dresser.

My mother stands behind me and twines a strand of my hair around her finger. "You don't need peroxide to make yourself beautiful. You already are." She grabs a brush off the dresser and begins brushing my hair. "Alice Carpenter is an ancestor you can be proud of. Look at what she did. After her husband dies, in 1623 she gets on this rickety ship, leaving her two boys with her sister, and sails across a huge ocean to get to America."

"Great. She leaves her children behind so she can marry someone else's husband," I say.

"Well," my mother says. "It wasn't her fault Dorothy May jumped off the Mayflower."

"Yeah, but it was William Bradford's fault for still being in love with Alice when he married Dorothy May."

"People can't help who they love. You'll see when you get older." She divides my hair into three sections and gently starts braiding them into one thick braid. "Just know that your father and I will accept anyone you love. As long as he's a Yankee fan."

"William never should have married Dorothy May in the first place and dragged her off to America. He was probably mean to her the whole trip because he was thinking about Alice. What a stupid man!" This is so dumb. I'm starting to yell about something that happened a long time ago.

My mother puts her arm around me. "Are you all right, Allie?"

"I'm fine. It's just so sad and stupid. I wish you had never told me that story." I turn away so she can't see my eyes watering up.

"Did something happen today? Something with Marissa? She hasn't been around here much lately." She has that concerned-mother sound in her voice.

"Nothing's wrong." I start to leave, but she holds onto my arm.

"I know eighth grade can be hard," Mom says. "Girls especially can be pretty mean to each other. Every day girls cry in my office because they've been excluded from some clique."

"I'm not crying to you." I pull my arm away.

"I know. I've always been glad I haven't had to worry about seeing you in my office." She tries to put her arm around me; I shrug it off. "When I was in eighth grade, the group I was in split up and some of us didn't speak again until our twentieth high-school reunion."

"You've only told me that fifty billion times." I used to like hearing stories of when my mother was a kid. Now I don't want to hear them.

"Well, I just don't think things change all that much. I treated my mother pretty much the same way you treat me."

"What are you talking about?" I hate when she tries to compare me to her when she was my age. I'm nothing like the way she was. She was totally into boys and is always asking me if I have a crush on someone.

"I was embarrassed by her, too." Mom kisses the top of my head. I pull away from her and walk towards the door.

"All right. I'll save my smooches for when I tuck you in tonight." She puts that sad look on her face. Like I'm supposed to run to her like I used to and say, "You're the best Mommy."

"You don't really need to do that. I'm thirteen years old," I say, stopping at the door.

"Too bad. I'm going to do it until you're fifty."

"I won't be living here."

"You never know. I read in the newspaper that kids graduating from college are starting to move back in with their parents."

"Shoot me if I do that."

"No. I'll just charge you rent."

3

At my desk, I leaf through the binder labeled "My Pilgrim Ancestors" that my mother gave me. I stare at the dates. My ancestor William Bradford lived from 1590 to 1657. He was governor of the Plymouth colony for thirty years with his second wife, Alice Carpenter, by his side. And his first wife, poor Dorothy May, lived from 1597 to 1620. So she was only twenty-three when she died. That's so young. She didn't have a chance to do anything with her life.

But how does this all relate to me? And how am I going to use it to write a paper about my family tree? All I can think of is my life with all the lonely days stretching out before me without Marissa—all the lunchtimes I'll have to sit by myself in the cafeteria, all the cell-phone minutes I won't need because I'll have no one to call.

I glance at the thumbtacked photos of Marissa and me on my bulletin board. There we are wearing mud-caked soccer uniforms, our arms around each other's shoulders; another with our hands on our hips, posing in our first bikinis. In a photo from kindergarten, Marissa swings from the monkey bars, her face flushed with the success of finally reaching the end in one try. And I stand underneath her, her shadow shading my face, my hands outstretched as if waiting for her to fall.

To escape from these pictures, I wander over to the window looking out over our backyard. Our old swing set, where Marissa once swung from the monkey bars, is black with mildew. And the pool where we spent our summers is now dotted with red and orange autumn leaves from the silver-maple trees that surround it. A blow-up whale floats by itself. When I open the window, a chilly breeze blows in.

Touching the tiny fairy charm on the chain around my neck, I read the inscription on the attached disk, "A&M: BFF." Instead of "Best Friends Forever," BFF could now mean "Better Find another Friend." Without thinking, I rip the necklace off my neck, and throw it out the window.

"Good-bye, little one." I watch the fairy make a tiny splash as she falls into the pool. But when I turn back to my homework, I begin to feel sorry for the poor little fairy with her tiny wings. How lonely she'll be at the bottom of the pool. I decide to rescue her; I sprint past my mother's room, down the stairs, past my brother who's still killing terrorists on his computer, and push open the screen door that leads out to our above-ground pool.

I climb the steps and kneel on the edge of the wooden deck surrounding the pool, watching out for splinters from the aging redwood. With both hands as if I'm doing the breaststroke, I push away the leaves and peer into the water. It's difficult to see the bottom with the leaves blocking the light, so I lean in further, almost pressing my face against the water.

Suddenly someone screams, *"Jump not!"* and I am pushed down on the pool deck. But it's as if a strong wind pushed me rather than a person.

"What are you doing?" I yell, as I try to catch my breath and roll myself into a sitting position. Standing over me is a young woman wearing an old-fashioned fitted jacket over a white shirt with a ruffled collar and a very long, full skirt. Her hair is covered by a white cap. She is very thin, and the fading sunlight shimmers on her skin making it seem transparent.

"Thou wast contemplating jumping into the water to drown thyself." She looks at me steadily, her grey eyes so serious as if she has never laughed. *"Thou art too young to take thy life."*

"I wasn't going to jump," I protest. "I was just trying to find the necklace I threw in the pool."

"No matter, thou may tell me the truth or not as thou wishes. Thy face was most sad. And I recognize that sadness. Once upon a time, that was upon my face." She speaks with an English accent, but not an upper-crusty kind like when you hear Prince Charles on television. It's more like the Beatles' accents, which I heard when my father made me watch *A Hard Day's Night.*

"Who are you?" I ask. "What are you doing here?"

"I am a friend come to be of assistance to thee. She holds out her hand, which I take and stand shakily, my legs still unsteady. *"When I espied thee close to the water, my worst fears were summoned."*

"But why are you wearing that Pilgrim costume?" Her shoes, which peek from underneath her long skirt, are pointed and narrow like the ones I've seen in books about Thanksgiving. These shoes, however, are worn and caked with mud. Then I think of the only person I know who is totally into Pilgrims. "Did my mother send you out here?"

"Thy mother?"

"Yeah, are you a member of one of those weird organizations that she's always talking about like Daughters of the Mayflower or something?" My mother told me about these people who dress up as Pilgrims and visit this fake Mayflower that's docked near Plymouth Rock.

"Indeed, I did journey to the New World in a ship by the name Mayflower. 'Twas the year of our Lord sixteen hundred and twenty." She states this as matter-of-factly as if she had said she was from New Jersey.

"Oh, sure. Where are my manners? Can I get you anything? Like a therapist?" I take her arm and try to lead her inside the house, but she resists. "My mother can help you."

"If it pleases thee to converse with my person, then I pray thee leave go my arm," she says huffily, tearing her arm away from me and dusting off her sleeve as if I have made it dirty. *"It took me well on six months to make my waistcoat and gown. 'Tis mine only apparel. I shall not let thee destroy it."*

"You made your outfit?" I notice that the long white apron over her green skirt is stained.

"Aye. 'Tis our custom to make one's clothing. Else how wouldst we dress?" She looks me up and down. *"I was compelled to save thee from drowning, but now that I am assured thou art safe, I shall be on my way."* She abruptly turns around and begins to walk away.

"Wait!" I call out. "Can you at least tell me your name?"

"Dorothy May," she says, but so softly that I wonder if it's the sound of the wind.

Something shiny catches my eye in the water and I grab the pool net to retrieve it. As I remove my necklace from the net, I look around for Dorothy May. But she has disappeared.

4

Alice Toth
Class: English: Mr. Sampson

FAMILY TREE PROJECT

I am descended from the Pilgrims, the people who landed on Plymouth Rock. Plymouth Rock is in Massachusetts, and there's not much left of it from people taking pieces of it.

The Pilgrims came from a village called Scrooby in England. (Don't get them confused with the Puritans, which is the name of the bigger group of Protestants the Pilgrims split off from.) The Pilgrims were part of a sect called "Separatists" because they separated from the Church of England and created their own religion. This was against the law so they had to escape to Holland. Then in 1620, they got on a boat called the Mayflower and came to America.

Then they were happy, except for the people who died because of the cold and disease the first winter after they landed. And this one woman, Dorothy May, was so unhappy she jumped off the Mayflower and drowned when the Pilgrims got to America, but before they stepped on Plymouth Rock.

I am descended from William Bradford, who became the governor of Plymouth for thirty-five years, and his second wife, Alice Carpenter, who I am named after. She came over on a boat called the Anne in 1623 to marry William Bradford after Dorothy May, his first wife, jumped off the Mayflower.

⧽⊲⊳⧼

When I get my paper back, it has a note from Mr. Sampson. *Allie, this is a nice beginning. I am intrigued with the story of Dorothy May. But I want you to dig deeper. Connect with Dorothy May. Find out what makes her tick. By the way, I am also descended from the Pilgrims. My ancestors are Priscilla Mullins and John Alden, who met on the Mayflower.*

Oh, great. Mr. Sampson is an ancestry maniac like my mother. I don't get it. What's so interesting about a bunch of dead people? Can they help me do my homework or hang out with me when Marissa is off with her new friends? And now Mr. Sampson wants me to "connect" with Dorothy May? We barely speak the same language. She uses all those thee's and thou's. I don't think the Pilgrims were even allowed to dance, and the clothes they wore were so gloomy—all that black and grey. Yuck.

And I used to really like Mr. Sampson. Everyone wants to be in his class. On the blackboard, he drew this "What Fools These Mortals Be" Idiot Meter, and every time somebody says something stupid, he draws a line to show it rising. Like the time Mathew Huddle hadn't read *Romeo and Juliet* and said it was a comedy because it ended happily.

Mr. Sampson had raised his eyebrows and said, "I don't know about you, but when two young kids kill themselves with poison and a knife stabbing, I don't consider that a happy ending. But maybe it's that violent Japanese animation you all watch." And he drew a line to show the Idiot Meter rising. He says if we get to the top, we'll have one class where all our answers should be wrong.

I try to catch Marissa as she leaves Mr. Sampson's class, but she practically flies out of the room. I find her hanging out at Crystal's locker, laughing hysterically like Crystal's some brilliant comedian, when we all know Crystal is as funny as spilled nail polish. How could Marissa possibly find anything to talk about with Crystal and Suzanne? In Spanish class in elementary school, they never knew the answers to any of the teacher's questions, so Marissa and I called them Dumbo Uno and Dumbo Dos.

"Hi, Marissa." I plant myself in front of her so she can't run away. She's wearing yet another new outfit—a short pink skirt with a lighter pink stretchy top. Long ago, Marissa told me that pink was her "signature" color. Crystal's outfit matches Marissa's, as does her shade of blonde hair. I wonder how Marissa feels about someone horning in on her signature color. But then I get a sinking feeling. Maybe they planned it.

"Hi, Allie," Marissa says. "You get home okay yesterday?"

"Yeah, I walked." I shrug as if it was no big deal, even though it took me over an hour. Well, at least she cares, I think.

Marissa starts to turn back to Crystal, then stops. "Those my jeans?" she asks, staring at my new low-cut jeans.

"No, my mom bought them for me. Can you believe she finally let me have a pair? You know how she's always saying, 'First comes the sexy jeans. Then the sex.'" My laugh comes out sounding too loud.

"How queer," Crystal says, smirking at Marissa.

Marissa nods, then says to me, her voice cold, "I need my jeans back, the ones you wore yesterday."

"Sure. Do you want to come over after school and get them?" I try to smile at her like we're still best friends, but she doesn't smile back.

"She's coming to my house," Crystal says. She slits her eyes really small probably to show off her silver eye shadow.

"Well, I could bring them there." Why do I sound like I'm begging? I feel like screaming at Crystal, "This is my best friend! Not yours!" She's only been friendly with Marissa for a couple of weeks.

"I don't think so," Crystal says. "We're doing a project together."

"Oh, I didn't think you were in any of the same classes." How could they be? Marissa was in advanced classes like me. Crystal was probably taking classes like "Math You Should have Learned in Third Grade" or "English Grammar: What's a Vowel?"

"This project isn't for school," Marissa says. "I'm helping Crystal highlight her hair." Crystal fluffs up her white-blonde hair like she thinks she's a movie star. A couple of boys walk by her and drool.

"Oh," I say. "Well, good luck."

"Good luck? Why would we need luck to highlight my hair?" Crystal asks, and Marissa laughs with a high-pitched shriek. I guess "good luck" was a pretty stupid thing to say, but I can't talk normally around Marissa anymore.

5

When I sit down with my journal after school and try to "connect" with Dorothy May, everything sounds so stupid. *"Where did you hang out?* We hang out at the mall. *Did you have a pet?* We have a dog. He's always stealing food off the counter. *Was your mother obsessed with genealogy websites, too?"* But then I realize that's dumb—they didn't have computers in the seventeenth century.

What I really want to ask Dorothy May is, *"Did you have a best friend? Did she dump you in eighth grade leaving you with no friends?"*

Could that really have been the ghost of Dorothy May by the pool last night? No one will ever believe me. I can hardly believe it and I was there. What does she do? Go around saving people she thinks are going to drown themselves. I decide I'd better ask my mother more about Dorothy May.

When I enter the kitchen, Dad is launching into his usual, "Can't we ever have a home-cooked meal, Pam?"

He's wearing his favorite t-shirt that reads, "My Kids Think I'm Great!" It's really faded because we gave it to him for Father's Day a long time ago.

My mother's at the table, the grey streak in her hair falling in her face. She looks up from the book she's reading, *The Descendants of William Bradford.* "You should have married Julia Child," she says to my father.

"And you should have married someone who loves microwave dinners." He pokes at the chicken enchilada in the plastic container in front of him.

"Hey, Dad, there's no warning label on cookbooks that says, 'For Women Only,'" I say, scooping kibble into Laszlo's dish. Dad insisted that since Mom got to name my brother and me after her ancestors, he could give the dog a Hungarian name after his. Laszlo is a big black-and-white mutt who sleeps all day, which Dad says is very fitting since most of Dad's relatives are the same way.

"You know, Allie, when I met your mother, she used to make me four-course dinners." Dad rubs the bald spot on the top of his head, like he's Aladdin rubbing his magic lamp and wishing for a gourmet meal. My brother Will scoots in, grabs his pizza bagel out of the toaster oven, and runs off to Alex's house to do homework.

"If I kept that up, Doug, you'd be 300 pounds." Mom playfully pokes Dad in the stomach with her finger.

"See, Mom's doing you a favor." I plop down at the table in front of my microwave mac and cheese.

"Oh well, I guess I should consider myself lucky that your mother let me mix with her illustrious gene pool." He points to the book she's reading about William Bradford.

"My ancestors are probably rolling in their graves knowing I married a Hungarian." She leans over and gives Dad a kiss on the cheek.

Before they can get all mushy, I spot my opening to ask Mom about Dorothy May. "Oh, Mr. Sampson liked my paper on my Mayflower Family Tree."

"I hope you told them about the distinguished ancestors you have on my side," my father says. "About your brave Hungarian great-grandfather who won a medal for leading a retreat, bravely running away from the enemy."

"No, I wrote about Mom's Pilgrim ancestors this time. And Mr. Sampson wanted to know more about Dorothy May." I stir the liquid cheese with my fork.

"Dorothy May?" My mother narrows her eyes. "Your ancestor is Alice Carpenter. Dorothy May isn't even related to you. Why would you want to write about someone who killed herself?"

"I don't know." I wish I hadn't brought it up. My mother is so protective about her heritage. She wants to believe that all her ancestors are distinguished, even one who was only related through marriage. "I guess...I guess because she was interesting."

"And that's the only reason? You weren't interested in her because she committed suicide?" My mother pushes her glasses up on her nose and peers into my eyes like she's trying to psychoanalyze me.

"No, I'm not interested in her because of that." Jeez. First Dorothy May and now my mother think I'm going to kill myself.

"Well, I hope you'll tell Mr. Sampson that you're not related to her," she says in a huff.

"Fine, fine. I'll tell him." Because my mother is being so sensitive on this subject, I take a deep breath before asking, "But I did want to ask you something. You said that Dorothy May killed herself because William Bradford was still in love with Alice Carpenter, right?"

"Yes, that's true, but there were probably other factors." She fiddles with her knife as she thinks. "For instance, she had just undertaken a very difficult journey—it was extremely cold and wet, and the food was rotten. And she missed her little son who she had left behind in Holland."

"She did? How old was he?"

"Three."

"That's terrible."

"Yes. But despite all that, a completely sane person doesn't usually kill herself." She holds up her knife for emphasis.

"Oh, so what was wrong with her?"

"Well, if I had to make a guess, she probably had bipolar disorder."

"Bipolar disorder?" I ask.

"Yeah, she could have had mood swings. I imagine sometimes she would be extremely happy, but then that might lead to a huge drop in her emotions where she'd be extremely sad." She has that official school-psychologist tone in her voice. "At the time, they might have said she was 'plagued by ill humors.'"

"Oh," I say.

"But I hope you're not going to put this in your paper as if it's a fact," my mother says. "This is just conjecture."

"Oh, I would never do that," I say, crossing my fingers under the table. Because that is exactly what I plan on doing.

6

After dinner, I turn on the water in the bathtub. I figure I'll complete the Dorothy May assignment after a long soak in the tub, which I really need after all that's happened lately. But before I put my toe in the water, I hear the words, *"Jump not!"* And I turn around to see Dorothy May appearing out of the steam.

"You again! First you imagine I'm drowning myself in my pool and now you think I'm going to kill myself by jumping into two inches of bath water." I wrap my robe more tightly around myself.

"Thou needs be most careful around water." She hesitantly touches the water gushing out of the faucet, but draws her hand back quickly. *"Might this be witchcraft?"* she gasps.

"No," I say. "Most people have a bathtub like this in their house, if not two or three. And this isn't even a fancy one."

"I cannot imagine where thy father finds such abundant wood by which to stoke the fire for so many baths. He must chop down a forest." Her eyes open wide.

"He doesn't have to chop anything down. The water comes to us automatically through pipes." I turn the water up higher so more gushes out. "There's always plenty."

"Thou art most fortunate," she says. *"On the Mayflower, 'twas no spare water for washing, and we were crowded together below deck for two long months. If thou wast not already sick from the storms tossing the ship nearly upside itself or the infestation of insects, the stench would make thee so."* She hides her hands beneath her apron, but not before I see that her fingernails are dirty. And now that she and I are in close quarters, I notice a pungent smell coming from her.

"Here, you can have the bath. I can take one tomorrow night." I gesture towards the bathtub.

"I do not wish to take a thing which is thine."

"I'm so tired, I'd probably fall asleep in the tub. Come on." I take her hand. "Take a bath. It'll make you feel less depressed."

"De-pressed. 'Tis an unfamiliar word."

"Never mind. It's not a very helpful word." If she is bipolar like my mother suggested, I don't want to make her feel more depressed by telling her what it means. Instead, I demonstrate how to turn on the hot and cold water, and I pour in the pink liquid bubble bath.

She jumps back when the water starts to foam. *"Art thou certain 'tis not a potion what will transform me into a cat or some such thing?"*

"I promise. You will turn into nothing but clean." I hand her a fluffy yellow towel. She rubs her face in it, inhaling the floral scent of the laundry detergent.

"Well, enjoy your bath," I tell Dorothy May, and she smiles. As I close the door to the bathroom and head for bed, I imagine her soaking in the hot tub, the sparkling bubbles washing away centuries of dirt.

7

Alice Toth
Class: English: Mr. Sampson

DOROTHY MAY FROM THE MAYFLOWER

Last night, one thing I learned from Dorothy May is that the passengers on the Mayflower were really dirty because they couldn't take baths for two months. And they didn't have bathtubs in those days with running water.

Dorothy May seems like a very nice person. I can't tell if she knows I'm related to the woman her husband was in love with. I don't really feel I know her well enough yet to tell her.

I think the reasons Dorothy May might have jumped off the Mayflower were: 1. Her husband was in love with someone else. 2. There were bugs in the meat she was eating. 3. She had to leave her son behind in Holland. 4. She was very cold from the snow and the icy rain. (It was December in Cape Cod. You can imagine how cold that would be.) 5. The cabin she was staying in was packed with smelly people because no one could take a bath. 6. My mother, who is a psychologist, says Dorothy probably had bipolar disorder, but they wouldn't have known that then because psychologists weren't invented yet.

~≈⋈≈~

While I read to the class from my journal, Mr. Sampson nods a lot and rubs his light brown buzz-cut, which he does when he likes what he hears. My face feels sunburn hot and my voice is so high it sounds like someone tuning a violin. When I finish, I close my journal and take deep gulps of air to try to calm down. I catch Marissa's eye and smile sheepishly. She gives me a half smile back, which is a good sign, I think. She must have highlighted her hair along with Crystal's yesterday because it looks lighter.

"Allie, that is a good example of combining historical facts with imagining what happened." Mr. Sampson jumps up from his seat and bounds to the blackboard. He pulls a piece of chalk from his back pocket and writes: "Fact: Dorothy May jumped off the Mayflower. Conjecture: Why she jumped."

He spins his short, wiry body around a few times with his eyes closed and his arm extended. When he stops, his finger is pointing at Josh Bryce, one of the only cool guys in our class.

"Okay Josh," Mr. Sampson says. "Tell us why this fact and this conjecture make an interesting journal entry."

Josh combs his fingers through his wavy dark-brown hair as if stalling for time. Everyone loves Josh. He's one of those kids who can fit in with anyone. He's a good athlete, but he doesn't take it too seriously. He gets good grades, but he doesn't stress about it. He's tall and skinny, but even though he has long legs, he takes his time ambling down the hall so he can smile at everyone. And it doesn't hurt that he's really cute in a non-scary way. Like he's not so good-looking that you can't talk to him.

"Because Allie's smart and everything she writes is interesting," Josh says, tapping a pencil on his desk. The class laughs, then they all turn to see how I'm reacting. I look down so they can't see my goofy grin.

"Not the answer I was looking for, you brown-noser. Are you by any chance running for class president again this year?" Mr. Sampson takes a couple of big strides over to Josh's desk to stand over him and peer down like he's a strict task-master.

"Of course." Josh smiles up at Mr. Sampson. "How else can I get rid of all these leftover 'Josh Bryce for President' pencils?" He hands Mr. Sampson his pencil. Mr. Sampson pretends that when he tries to write with it, it doesn't work, so he tosses it like he's throwing a basketball.

"Two points!" Mr. Sampson exclaims when it lands in the trash can. He crosses his arms and leans back on his heels. "All right, Sports Fans, Allie is starting from a unique premise—that her Pilgrim was a real person with her own problems, not just a noble symbol of our country that we trot out at Thanksgiving. So I, for one, would like to hear more. Allie, keep writing about your friend Dorothy May."

"She's not my friend," I say. "She's just someone I picked out of history." Everyone would think I was crazy if I said Dorothy really existed.

"Well, if the rest of your final project is as good as this, it's a slam-dunk 'A' for sure." Mr. Sampson pretends he's dribbling a basketball and throws it to me. He says that basketball is the sport of the gods—the ancient gods, that is. He doesn't want to get into trouble for bringing talk of religion into the schools.

"My great-grandfather was a bank robber," Mathew Huddle calls out in his squeaky voice. "Can I write about him?" Once again, Mathew is copying me. Figures, the only boy who has ever liked me has bad body odor. My mother says he probably just has overactive sweat glands, but she doesn't have to sit next to him five days a week.

"Sure, Mathew," Mr. Sampson says. "Just as long as you realize that bank robbery is not a valid career path for you to take. I don't want your mother calling me to say I'm encouraging the wrong values."

"I'm sorry she called you about the Idiot Meter." Mathew takes off his glasses and starts rubbing the lenses with his shirt like he always does when he's nervous. "I wouldn't have told her about it, except I thought she'd think it was funny."

"There's no predicting the sense of humor of a mother," Mr. Sampson says. "When I was a kid, I brought my mother breakfast in bed and put my hamster inside the sugar bowl. I thought it was hysterical. She wasn't amused."

The students start shouting out questions like "What did your mother do?" and "Did the hamster eat the sugar?" We all love hearing stories about Mr. Sampson when he was a kid. He was always getting into trouble.

But the bell rings. "Ah, that is for another day," Mr. Sampson says, erasing the board. "See you tomorrow. 'Parting is such sweet sorrow.' I'll award the rubber chicken to the first person who can tell me what play that quote is from."

"*Romeo and Juliet*," I blurt out without thinking.

"Coming at you, Allie." Mr. Sampson throws me the rubber chicken. "Parting is such sweet sorrow that I shall say good night till it be morrow."

Marissa and a couple of other girls glare at me. Between Mr. Sampson's positive comments on my paper and being awarded the rubber chicken, I had definitely reached my daily quota of compliments from the teacher.

At the end of the day, I wait to see if Marissa will meet me at my bus and come home with me like she used to. But then I see Marissa get on Crystal's bus. They look like two pink glamour girls with matching blonde hair. I guess Marissa really wanted someone for a best friend who looked like her. She used to ask me to dress like her, too, but my mother told me we couldn't afford it. "Her mother never buys anything on sale," Mom said. "She doesn't have to. She married for money."

8

That night as I try to fall asleep, I can't get the image of Marissa leaving with Crystal after school out of my head. It's Friday night, the night Marissa used to sleep over at my house in the identical bed across from mine. Like everything else in the house, these beds are antique, but I kind of like them anyway. They belonged to my great-great-grandmother. She lived on a farm in Illinois and the tiger-maple bedposts are carved into the shape of corncobs. Sometimes at night, I imagine my ancestor falling asleep in one of these beds, exhausted after a day of milking cows and planting corn.

I pick up the water bottle I keep on the nightstand next to my bed. Mom started leaving a water bottle there when I was younger to stop me from calling out for a drink of water. As soon as I take my first sip, Dorothy May shimmers into being before me. She looks cleaner this time. Her fingernails aren't dirty.

I'm so surprised that water spurts out of my mouth. "You can't be thinking I'm going to jump into this bottle of water?" I wipe my wet chin with the sheet.

"Nay," she says quietly, *"though I do think water summons me."*

"Oh, is that because you jumped into water?" I ask.

"What?" Her voice is just above a whisper.

"Well, you know, you jumped off the Mayflower into Provincetown Harbor. Maybe that's why you're attracted to water."

Dorothy May trembles. Her face turns white. *"I did hope the ship's captain would report that I fell from the Mayflower; that 'twas a mishap."* She peers into my eyes as if pleading for me to change what I just said.

"In most history books, it says that you accidentally slipped off the deck of the ship." I choose my words carefully. I don't want to hurt her feelings, but I also feel that I must tell the truth, or we'll never figure out why she came to see me, or how I can help her. "But my mother showed me a book that says you jumped on purpose, although it's hard to know for sure because your body was never found."

"It fills me with sorrow to hear that my death was regarded a suicide." She bows her head as if praying. *"In our church, 'tis a sin to take one's life."* Her shoulders hunch and her head falls forward onto her chest, tears falling from her eyes.

"Oh, I'm sorry." I jump out of bed, and take her hand. It is tiny, but rough as if she's washed a lot of dishes. "I didn't mean to make you cry." As I sit her down on the edge of my bed, I smell soap on her skin, a nice change from last night.

"Did you enjoy your bath?" I ask, trying to change the subject.

"Indeed. I thank thee for that. I believe it warmed my soul." She wipes her eyes with her sleeve, which is torn and frayed.

"We should get you into some clean clothes."

"These are mine only garments. I was married in these self-same clothes." Dorothy points to her long, green wool dress with an off-white petticoat peeking out the bottom along with a pair of thick stockings.

"Did you have a big wedding?" I ask.

"Nay. 'Twas a simple ceremony, though I was most proud to have William Bradford by my side whilst the minister announced our names from the pulpit upon three Sundays." Her grey eyes light up. *"Is that the way people marry today?"*

"No, they have big weddings where they invite hundreds of people, and their wedding gown costs thousands of dollars. And if their parents are divorced, they fight over who's going to sit at the bride and groom table. That's what happened at my cousin's wedding."

"I would not desire a wedding such as that." Dorothy sits with her back straight as a rod. *"I was a shy girl of but sixteen years with few relations and fewer friends."*

"We dream about our wedding day our whole life," I tell her. "We play with bride dolls and dress up in bride costumes." I open my closet and show Dorothy a box containing my old Barbie doll dressed as a bride.

"She is quite beautiful" Dorothy gently touches Barbie's veil.

"You can have her if you want. I have a million Barbie dolls. My Mom's anti-Barbie, so everyone else's mother felt sorry for me and gave them to me for birthday presents." Sadly, I remember Marissa and I playing Barbies when we were younger, pretending our dolls were on exotic fashion shoots in Hawaii.

"I thank thee," Dorothy says as I hand her the doll. She lifts Barbie's veil and strokes her long honey-blonde hair.

"Can I try something?" I ask.

"Will it hurt?" she asks. I shake my head as I stand her in front of the mirror. Then I start to take off her white cap.

"Oh, no!" she says. *"A virtuous woman must keep her hair under her coif."*

"I promise I won't tell anyone. Especially not the Pilgrims."

She hesitates, but then nods and helps me remove the cap. I begin to brush her straight brown hair. I braid several ribbons into it. She smiles at herself in the mirror.

9

The next day is Saturday. "Rise and shine!" Dad stands in the doorway of my room and blows the whistle he's wearing around his neck. "It's a big day for the Bobcats. I just know we're going to win." He throws my soccer uniform at me. "Come on, princess. Your high-carb breakfast awaits you. Toast, toast, and more toast."

He's already dressed for assistant coaching with his khaki shorts and the torn-grey sweatshirt with the University of Connecticut logo on it. He bought it in college a million years ago and we've offered to buy him a new one, but he says this one gives him luck. I don't know what kind of luck it gives him since our team has won only one game this season.

"Go away!" I yell. "Don't you read *Parents* magazine? Kids are supposed to get ten hours sleep." I look at my Winnie the Pooh clock on the wall, which I should have replaced ages ago. It's only nine o'clock.

Dad sits on the edge of my bed and starts bouncing while singing a kids' song. "'A my name is Allie and my husband's name is Al. We come from Alabama just to bring you apples.' As well as a soccer ball and cleats," he adds. "If I have to get up for this game, so do you. You're the one who picked soccer."

"Only because you made me go out for a sport." I roll over and stuff my head under the pillow.

"You need to be a balanced kid. Have I ever told about the Greek ideal of a sound body and a sound mind?" He grabs the pillow, then flexes his muscles like a body builder.

"Only three hundred times."

"Hey, you don't want to be one of those kids with a gigantic head stuck on top of this puny little body because you study all the time and never exercise, do you?" He pulls the quilt off me.

"The soccer team will do fine without me. I'm so slow." I try to pull the quilt back on, but since he's stronger, he always wins at our game of quilt tug-of-war.

"You're actually very fast. Well, your upper body anyway. It's just that your feet haven't caught up yet." He grabs my feet and starts to pull me out of bed.

I look around for signs of Dorothy May, but all I see is the Barbie bride lying on the pillow beside me. Did Dorothy May put her there? Was she really here last night?

"Why won't you let me quit? I'm not any good at it, and this soccer uniform makes me look fat."

"Because I want to torture you." He starts tickling me. "I am a torture machine."

"Stop it," I say through my giggles. "It's not funny."

He gives me a quick kiss on the top of my head and starts to leave so I can get dressed. At the doorway, he turns and says, "Your foremothers fought for you to get the right to vote and play soccer. It's the least you can do to show your appreciation."

I wish they had fought for the right for me to get more sleep.

10

It's windy and cool when we get to the soccer field, but the sun is shining so it feels warm for a fall day. Marissa's already there, standing on the sidelines with her father. She looks bored without her new buddies. Crystal and Suzanne are probably at the mall getting pedicures.

The only reason Marissa still plays is the same reason I do; our fathers make us. They were both soccer stars in college and want us to love the game as much as they do.

"Hi," I say to Marissa as I throw down my soccer ball and water bottle next to her pink athletic bag. Her mother gets Marissa's soccer uniform taken in by a tailor so it fits her perfectly, showing off her long legs and tiny waist.

"You'll never know where a talent scout for models will discover you," her mother would say. I doubt it will be on this crummy soccer field with the empty beer cans left over from the high-school kids.

"I wonder if we'll win today." I sound like a dweeb so I add, "Not that I care, but it would sure make our dads happy."

Why does everything I say to Marissa these days sound like lines from a corny TV show? All I really want to say is, "Let's be friends again."

Marissa doesn't reply. She takes her soccer ball out of her bag and throws it on the ground. She kicks the ball back and forth between her insteps. Like the other girls around us, I start to stretch, pulling my right foot up to touch my back. I always feel like I'm going to fall on my face when I do this. I just about decide Marissa isn't going to speak to me, when she says, "I'm going to quit soccer." She's talking in a low voice and I realize she waited until her father walked away.

"Oh, yeah, me too," I say, happy that she's talking to me.

"I can't play this lame game forever. I make sure to show my mother all the bruises I get on my legs, so she'll freak and tell my Dad I should quit before this sport deforms my legs." She wraps an elastic band around her hair to pull it away from her face. The highlights look perfect, the blonde strands blending naturally with the brown hair underneath.

She turns away from me as if she's going to run over to another group of girls, so I quickly say, "What's happening with your modeling career?"

"My mother's getting a professional photographer to take pictures of me next week for my portfolio to take to her old modeling agency." She acts bored, but I know she's excited. She's been preparing for this moment her whole life. When we were little, we played fashion model. She'd be the model and I'd be the photographer.

"That's great. Your mom is finally letting you see if you can be a model." I kick my ball up, bouncing it several times on my thigh. I look up to see if Marissa's impressed with my juggling, but she's scouting the sidelines probably to see if any of the boys who come to watch us have noticed how great she looks. "Do you know what you're going to wear to the shoot?" I ask.

"Mom's going to take me shopping at her special store."

"Where she gets all her designer clothes?" I try not to sound eager. We used to talk about how I would go with Marissa to help pick out her clothes for her first modeling assignment. Maybe she'll remember and ask me.

"Yeah," she says. "Dad's trying to give her a budget."

"Like she ever pays attention to that." I laugh.

"Hey, don't make fun of my mother." She kicks her soccer ball across the field with an angry kick.

"I wasn't. We used to always say..." Could she really not remember how much we'd make fun of her mother's spending habits, calling her "Cruella de Ville with a credit card" because she was always coming home with a new fur coat? My stomach is beginning to hurt. Marissa's dad approaches.

"Are we ready to kick butt, Bobcats?" Like my father, Mr. Donnelly's got his Dad-coach outfit on—khakis and a college sweatshirt. He swipes at Marissa's ponytail playfully, but she jerks her head away. "Rumor has it the team we're playing is tough so we're going to need you on defense, Allie."

"All right, Mr. Donnelly." He smiles at me with his big goofy grin. I've heard my mother call Mr. and Mrs. Donnelly the princess and the frog because Mrs. Donnelly is so pretty, and Mr. Donnelly's eyes bulge out. But he's very nice.

"I haven't seen you around for awhile. What, you don't like my cooking?" Mr. Donnelly's cooking can be pretty bad—he's always experimenting.

"No, I love your food, Mr. Donnelly," I lie.

"Great. Then why don't you come over tonight? I'm making a new kind of burger. You chop up the cheese and put it inside before you grill it. I saw it on a cooking show." He pretends he's flipping a burger onto the clipboard he's holding.

Marissa looks down at the grass. She seems embarrassed. "Dad, I'm supposed to go to this dance with Crystal," she says through gritted teeth.

"Allie can go to the dance, too. Can't you, Allie?" He doesn't wait for an answer. "We'll see you at six-thirty. And don't forget to wear your dancing shoes." He blows the whistle. Marissa and her dad are encircled by fifteen girls in identical yellow shirts. I stand on the outside of the circle wondering if it's worth pushing my way in.

11

After I get home from soccer, I climb over our backyard fence. Connor McBride greets me at the door with a water pistol. He's about to press the trigger when Mrs. McBride snatches it from him.

"Give Allie a chance to take off her jacket," she says. "He's been counting the minutes until you got here. So have I. I still can't believe taking care of a three-year-old boy can be more stressful than managing an office of fifty people." Mrs. McBride pats Connor's messy blonde hair as he tries to grab the water pistol from her. She sweeps a brush through her sandy-blonde hair and pulls it back into what she calls her "busy-mom ponytail."

"Where's Marissa?" Mrs. McBride asks.

"Uh, she couldn't make it today." I avoid looking at her so she won't ask any more questions.

"I want Marissa," Connor whines. He thrusts out his lower lip as if he's about to cry. The last time Marissa babysat with me, she showed Connor how to hunt for bugs in the garden. They found a slug, which Connor named Elmo.

"Never mind, Connor. I'm sure you'll have fun with Allie." She gives him a big hug before she edges toward the door. "Ah, two blissful hours." She smiles broadly, tossing me the water pistol as she quickly opens the door and scoots out.

"I want water pistol." Connor lunges toward me, but I rush to the kitchen. "Come on, Connor. Let's see what great snacks your mother has." I throw open the snack cabinet and there they are—fabulous, loaded-with-sugar, totally bad-for-you snacks. I pull out a box of donuts.

"Don't you think donuts go much better with soda than milk?" I ask Connor as I open the refrigerator and grab a can of diet soda. "Oh, I'm in junk-food heaven."

"Want to play," yowls Connor. He grabs the water pistol from the counter. "Got you." As I turn toward him, he squirts me in the face with a long stream of water.

"Cut it out, Connor!" I grab a dishtowel to dry off my face. When I open my eyes, Dorothy May is standing next to Connor. I smile to think a stream of water from a water pistol can bring her here.

"He is most precious," she says.

"He's totally exhausting. You'll see."

"Want to play trains," Connor says, ignoring Dorothy May and dragging me toward his train set in the playroom.

"He doesn't seem to see you," I say to Dorothy May.

"It appears that thou art the only one who can."

Connor sets the red engine and the blue engine facing each other on the track and crashes them into each other. "Bam!" he says. "Allie, you be green one and I crash you."

"Connor, can't you let the trains go all around the track at least one time before you make them run into each other?" I start the green engine, but before it travels very far, Connor crashes into it with both the blue and the red engine.

"The child hast much vigor." She smiles at Connor and reaches out to stroke his hair. He stops for a moment and looks up as if he feels something, but then goes back to his trains. *"He brings to mind my son who would run by my side along the streets of Leiden."*

"Allie, can't find orange train." Connor grabs my hand and pulls me over to the toy box. "Orange train there." I start pulling out wooden train tracks and station houses. "Faster, Allie, faster," Connor says.

"Why couldn't Mrs. McBride have a girl who would play quietly with her dolls?" I ask.

"Ah, but he is a darling. Johnnie had curls like this one. How he would scream were I to put a brush to his hair."

"Why did you leave your son behind in Leiden?" I ask.

"Don't talk, Allie," Connor says. "Find orange train." When I finally retrieve it from the bottom of the toy box, Connor grabs it from my hand and runs over to the track.

"William did not believe our son would survive the voyage. He was but three years of age, you see." She grasps her arms tightly around herself as if holding a child.

"You must have missed your son so much."

"I would rather someone had cut off my arms than to have left my boy behind." She holds out her arms to me, and I notice how skinny they are. I remember how she said there was very little to eat on the Mayflower.

She kneels down beside Connor, who is now crashing the orange engine into the other ones. She stares at him with such sadness that I try to think of something to make her feel better. "You know, it's probably a good thing you didn't take your son on the Mayflower with you. My mother said that half the Pilgrims died that first year in Plymouth."

"I did not know that. Ah, perhaps William saved the life of our son by leaving him behind. Mayhaps 'twas I who was selfish to want him along on the voyage for I was as lonely as a pea separated from its pod." She stays rooted to the spot by Connor's side as if she's glued there.

"Didn't you have any friends to talk to?"

"Not a one. I was shy, you see, and not one to make friendships with ease. William was the one people would confide in. 'Twas no wonder he became a leader. If there were trouble aboard ship, William wouldst resolve it."

"My friend Marissa is like that, too. Everyone likes her better than me."

"Some day thou shalt find a worthy friend." She takes my hand and looks me in the eyes so that I'll believe her. Which I don't. My track record for making friends isn't especially promising.

Suddenly I hear a yelp and turn to see Connor throwing his train across the room. I run to pick him up as tears flood down his face. "What happened Connor?"

"Hurt finger. Bad train." He shows me his finger, which has a little cut on it. It must have gotten in the way when he was crashing trains together.

"Oh, poor Connor. Let's go find a bandage." I start to carry him toward the bathroom.

"Cobwebs," says Dorothy May.

"Cobwebs?"

"'Twill stop the bleeding. 'Tis a good thing his mother is not a proper housekeeper for I see one upon the curtain. Press it to the wound."

Despite my fear of spiders, I pull the cobweb off the curtain and wrap it around his finger. It stops the bleeding. I sit down in an over-stuffed chair and cuddle Connor, holding onto him tightly.

When I look up, I see that Dorothy is standing next to us with tears in her eyes, holding his hands in hers. Connor seems soothed by this and stops crying. *"I remember when tiny hands such as these helped me to stir the porridge."* She rubs Connor's back using a circular motion. Connor smiles.

"I guess you still have that mother's touch," I say.

"'Twould seem that way," she says, smiling sweetly.

12

I rush home from babysitting to find an outfit. I'm nervous about going to Marissa's house tonight. I can't believe I'll be in high school next year; my clothes are so middle school. Maybe if I cut off the bottom of one of my t-shirts so my stomach shows, it'll look cute. Out of my drawer, I pull a t-shirt I bought in Cape Cod when my family went on vacation there last summer. While we swam in the ocean, my mother traipsed through cemeteries tracking down the graves of her Pilgrim ancestors.

As I begin to cut the fabric, I sense someone watching me. When I look up, Dorothy May is standing there. That's when I notice that the design on the t-shirt is a Cape Cod beach scene with ocean waves crashing in the background.

Dorothy May's long brown hair is loose and falls past her shoulders.

"You're not wearing your cap," I say.

"I did not realize the weight my coif placed upon my head until thou set me free of it." She combs her fingers through her

hair, then delightedly tosses her head back so that her hair whips around, and she catches a glimpse of herself in the mirror above my dresser. *"I am not as pretty as some. 'Twas my fate to be plain, I suppose."*

I study the face that she calls plain. It's probably not a beautiful face by today's standards. Her lips are a little too thin and her brown hair is stringy. She could use a little eye shadow to bring out her grey eyes. Dorothy May's skin is her best feature. Milky white and completely smooth. Her skin is what saves her from being plain.

"You look a lot better than the Pilgrims in my books," I say. "They're always wearing that dreary black and white."

"Perchance thou art reading the wrong books." She steps lightly over to my bookshelf. *"Wouldst thou show me?"*

"All right." I find a book my mother gave me and flip to a painting of a Pilgrim woman.

Dorothy stares at the painting. *"'Tis true. Her clothing is drab."* She holds out the hem of her skirt. *"But as thou canst observe, my gown is green. We womenfolk dressed in all manner of colors—reds and yellows and browns. Aye, one time I owned a gown of a most striking violet."* She smiles like a little girl talking about her favorite doll.

My mother calls up the stairs, "Allie, you're going to be late!"

"Oh, Dorothy, I've got to go." I finish snipping off the bottom of the t-shirt and throw it over my head. The way the shirt hangs on me, I almost look cool.

Dorothy frantically yanks the shirt down to try and cover my bellybutton. *"Dost thou wish to be thrown in the stocks for dressing in so indecent a manner?"*

"They would do that just for dressing like this?"

"Indeed. With a paper pinned to thy hat with the words, 'obscene and lascivious' penned upon it." She finds the extra

piece of material I had cut off the t-shirt, and tries to reat-tach it. "Hast thou needle and thread?"

"Don't worry. Lots of kids cut their t-shirts. See." From the end of my bed, I grab a copy of *Teen People* magazine and hand it to her.

Opening it, she gasps, *"Art these witches? Nakedness is a sin."* She flings down the magazine as if it were burning her.

"They're not naked." I pick up the lip-gloss from the top of my dresser and smooth it across my lips. "This is just the way girls dress now. I mean, it's been almost four hundred years since you were a teenager. Things change."

"I am certain we shall find another garment for thee." She rifles through my closet, which is stuffed with clothes. *"Art thou of noble birth? Thou possess such beautiful clothing."* She touches the sleeve of the velvet gown I wore to my cousin's wedding.

"No," I laugh. "I'm just an ordinary girl. Too ordinary. If I were a princess, Marissa wouldn't leave me for new friends."

"I shall be thy friend," she says firmly. *"How well I remem-ber the feeling of being without companionship. 'Tis a most desolate sensation."*

"Thanks. I sure could use one. And I have something I can do for you. Here." I tug the velvet gown off its hanger and wrap it around Dorothy's shoulders like a shawl.

"'Tis not permitted in my church to wear something so friv-olous." But she folds her hands into the soft material.

"Allie!" my mother yells. "I'm leaving without you!"

"You'll be a lot more comfortable if you change into that dress." As I grab my coat out of the closet, I spot a pair of old Snow White slippers, which are too small for me, but might fit Dorothy's feet. "And these will make you feel cozy." I hand them to her.

"Where art thou going?" Dorothy asks as she smiles at the face of Snow White on the slippers.

"To Marissa's house."

"The same Marissa who hast left thee for new friends?"

I take one last glance in the mirror. "Her father invited me over tonight, but I just know if I have a chance to see Marissa by herself, we could be friends again."

"I pray thy hopes are not in vain. As much as I would not wish it to be so, one should not place thy trust in all people."

As I dash down the stairs, I hope that Dorothy May is wrong about my friendship with Marissa.

13

Mr. Donnelly's cheeseburgers turn out better than most of his concoctions. It's warm enough for us to sit outside on the deck in the white wicker chairs, although soon it'll be time for the Donnellys to stack them in the shed for the cold weather.

"Tell me, Allie, what's going on at your house?" Mrs. Donnelly tilts her chin up to get the most flattering light on her face, a technique she learned when she was a model. She's wearing white pants and a sailor top as if she's about to step onto a cruise ship. She wouldn't be caught dead in the sweatsuits my mother wears.

"My house?" I glance over at Marissa who coughs after taking a sip of lemonade. "Well, my mother traced one branch of our family tree to the Pharaohs. She thinks we could be related to King Tut."

Mr. Donnelly laughs, crinkling up his eyes till they seem to disappear. "That's certainly more interesting lineage than mine—a couple of drunken Irish kids on a broken-down farm in County Cork." He hands me a burger, practically burned to a crisp, the way I like it.

"Now, Ted," Mrs. Donnelly breaks in. "You don't know that that's your heritage. You haven't tried to trace it. Anyway, on my side of the family we have an English coat of arms." She sips her martini and delicately wipes her lips with a flowered cloth napkin.

"Yeah, didn't you order that by sending in two cereal box tops and a check for $4.99?" He winks. "Right, Marissa?"

"Don't ask me. I don't even know what a coat of arms is." She sneaks her burger into her lap to give to Bernie, their Tibetan Terrier. This is her old trick when she doesn't want to eat her father's food.

Mr. Donnelly tugs on his ear like he always does when he's about to tell us something educational. "A coat of arms is a family emblem handed down since the Middle Ages to identify a particular family. It might have a lion or a bear pictured on it to show how powerful the family was. I think mine has a chicken on it." He flaps his arms like they're wings. "Cluck, cluck."

"Stop, it, Ted," scolds Mrs. Donnelly, as if he was a child. "You're making it sound like Marissa's descended from failures, whereas my family has many illustrious ancestors." She points to the dishes we're using. "This china was handed down to me from my great-grandmother whose husband was a senator."

I feel the tiny raised fruits on the rim of my plate. Mrs. Donnelly uses her fine china even for outdoor dinners. She used to say, "My mother saved her china for special occasions. But those occasions never happened."

Just as I take another bite of my burger, Mrs. Donnelly asks, "So, Allie, how's your room coming along?"

"My room?" I almost choke.

"Yes, Marissa tells me she's helping you redecorate."

What is she talking about? I haven't redecorated since Mom finally replaced my Cinderella bedspread two years ago. Not to mention that Marissa hasn't been to my house since the summer. I try to catch Marissa's eye, but she's staring down at her plate.

"But I don't know if I really believe she's spending all that time at your house helping you redecorate," Mrs. Donnelly says. Marissa's head snaps up; her eyes are wary. "Allie, I'm beginning to think she has a crush on your brother." She smiles over at Mr. Donnelly who balls up his fist and punches it against his hand. He used to say he would challenge any boy who wanted to date Marissa to an arm wrestle.

"Ugh," I say. "I don't think so."

"Well, then what are you two doing over there all the time?" she asks.

I see Marissa looking at me intently. She's obviously been lying to her mother, telling her she was coming to my house when she was really somewhere else. But where?

"Yeah, well I guess Marissa and I, we just have a lot of fun together. You know, like we always have." I try to smile casually so they won't know I'm lying. Marissa looks relieved.

"You girls have been friends forever." Mrs. Donnelly takes my hand in hers. "I remember when Marissa came home from kindergarten and told us she had met a new friend who was really good on the monkey bars."

"She was really good," Marissa says.

"I had practiced all summer so I could swing all the way across the monkey bars on my first day." I can remember Marissa with a pink headband in her soft blonde hair. Even then, pink was her signature color. Marissa approached me and said, "You have to teach me how to do that." I taught her how to swing from the monkey bars, and she taught me how to hunt for bugs.

"Well, it's nice you two are still friends." Mrs. Donnelly takes Marissa's hand so that she's linking us together, holding my hand with one hand and Marissa's with her other. "I still have one really good friend from elementary school who means the world to me. When you're older, you'll be thankful you're still friends. You'll have someone who can remember your past with you."

Marissa smiles at her mother, and so do I.

14

As soon as we get out of her dad's car, Marissa rolls down the top of her striped pink skirt so her stomach shows. It looks great—so flat and still tan from summer and with a waist as tiny as Barbie's. We start walking toward the Bristol Teen Center, the social hall our town built so that kids would have a place to go. Inside, a DJ spins music. It's oldies night, and I can hear "Thriller" blasting through the windows. Marissa stops to look around for Crystal and Suzanne. That's when I notice something new.

"When did you get a bellybutton ring?" I ask. She's wanted one for a long time.

"Last week." She sticks her pinkie through the ring. "Cool, huh?" She smiles a big, wide smile, but I realize it's not for me. Marissa just got her braces off, and she wants to show off her straight, white teeth to all the kids hanging out in front of the Teen Center.

"Yeah, but I thought your mom wouldn't let you," I say.

"She changed her mind when I showed her all the models that had them. Dad doesn't know, though. He'd have like a million panic attacks." Marissa scouts the cars entering the parking lot for signs of Crystal and Suzanne. "I knew they'd be late. It takes Suzanne forever to put on her make-up."

"She does wear a lot of make-up." Tonight I'm wearing light blue eye shadow to match my light blue t-shirt. I wonder if the Cape Cod t-shirt was the right thing to wear. It looks babyish next to Marissa's cropped Princeton t-shirt.

"But not too much make-up. Suzanne always looks great." Marissa takes lip-gloss out of her pocket and spreads it across her lips. They look shiny and red like she's just eaten a cherry lollipop. "All the guys love her."

I nod, but not very enthusiastically. I don't really want to talk about Suzanne.

"You don't think she's pretty?" Marissa asks in kind of a snotty way.

"Yeah, she's pretty."

"You think Crystal is prettier?" she asks.

"I don't know," I say. "Are you taking a 'pretty' survey or something?"

"No, what's with you?" She scrunches up her face at me.

"Nothing. It's just that you didn't used to care about this stuff so much." We hear some screaming and turn to see a group of girls standing near the soda table next to the entrance. They're shrieking and laughing, while they grab and push each other in a kidding-around way. Anything to get attention. The popular girls are always the loudest. I guess that's why Marissa fits in. She's always been outgoing.

"Well, everyone thinks Crystal's beautiful." Marissa takes a little mirror out of her pink-leather bag. She opens her eyes wide and smoothes the eyeliner under her eye. "I need a nose job," she announces.

"What are you talking about? Your nose is perfect!" I practically scream this at her.

"No, there's a little bump. Right there. See?" She points to the non-existent bump.

"I don't see it. You're nuts."

"You could be prettier, you know." She turns and looks at me as if she's one of those women at the make-up counters in department stores who assess your skin tones.

"If I straightened my hair. You've been telling me that forever." Even when we were kids, Marissa was always putting gel in my hair to get rid of the frizz.

"You have a pretty face. But your hair always looks a mess."

"Thanks."

"I'm just telling you as a friend. There's this place in the city that straightens hair. It takes like five hours, but it lasts for six months. I'll go with you, if you want."

"Five hours? That sounds like torture."

She looks away and says softly, "Yeah, but then Suzanne and Crystal might want to hang around with you."

"Maybe I don't want to hang around with them. Did you ever think of that?" The words fly out of my mouth probably because I've been thinking them for so long.

"Everyone likes them. That's why they're popular," Marissa says in a matter-of-fact way. "And because they're so thin. You know you could lose a couple of pounds." She pinches my waist to demonstrate my poundage.

I push her hand away. "Oh, now I'm fat, too."

"Everyone's fat at school. Well, except Crystal and Suzanne."

"And you," I add.

"Right. Because I have a secret way to lose weight," she whispers.

"What?" I ask.

She carefully opens the zipper of her leather bag and reveals what's hidden inside.

"Cigarettes?" I gasp. "You smoke?"

"Once in a while, to cut my appetite. You should try it." She quickly zips up the bag.

"My mother would kill me," I say. "You know how she cuts out pictures of cancerous lungs and tapes them to the refrigerator."

"Allie, you've got to stop worrying about what your mother thinks." She says this like she's a teacher giving me a lesson. When did Marissa get so bossy?

"I don't. I just…My mom said to say hi. I think…I think she misses you."

"Yeah. Tell her hi." She turns away like she doesn't care.

"Marissa. Um. Why did you tell your mother you were coming to my house all the time?" My voice sounds shaky, cracking on some of the words.

Marissa zips and unzips her bag a couple of times. "Well. She doesn't like me going to the mall."

"Is that where you go after school with Suzanne and Crystal?"

"Mostly."

"Is it fun?"

"Yeah. Sure. They know everybody. I've met so many cool guys." She looks dreamy as if she's thinking about one of them.

"Is it as much fun as when we…"

"Allie. I don't want to talk about it. Things are different now. We're not little kids anymore. We're in eighth grade." She flips her long hair.

"I just thought…"

"Oh, good. There's Suzanne and Crystal." She waves. "I love Crystal's skirt. She really knows how to dress."

Crystal's skirt looks pretty much like Marissa's and she has it rolled down the same way. They could almost be sisters now that Crystal has highlights the same color as Marissa's. They have the same blue eyes and perfect noses.

Suzanne's hair is dyed a really pretty black, which she wears in a long ponytail. Black eyeliner encircles her violet eyes and makes them stand out.

"I love your skirt," Marissa squeals as Crystal twirls around so everyone can see her short pink skirt, which is identical to Marissa's except it has pink ribbon sewn on the bottom. "Where'd you get it?"

"You missed a great shopping adventure today, Marissa," Suzanne says. "Like the jacket?" She models her green clingy jacket.

"Nice. You didn't…?" Marissa asks.

"Absolutely," Suzanne says proudly. "Five-finger discount. Practically right in front of a guard."

"They never suspect you're going to shoplift right in front of them." Crystal touches Marissa's bellybutton ring. "Ooh, that looks so cool."

Marissa taps Crystal's identical bellybutton ring. "Ooh, so does yours."

"Well, you missed it, Marissa," Suzanne says. "You had to spend your day being a soccer jock." She spits out the word "soccer."

"Yeah, well, Dad wouldn't let me miss the game," Marissa says. "We didn't even win."

"You guys never win. You might as well give it up. Besides, who wants to spend time bouncing balls off your head?" Crystal bangs her head against her palm. "Ouch," she says.

"Yeah, I still kind of have a headache after this morning's game," I say. "I headed a ball really hard. I made a goal, though."

Crystal doesn't even look at me. "Marissa, you have to join the lacrosse team. We have much cooler parties. All the cute boys come."

"And we don't let just anyone join." Suzanne fingers a lacrosse-stick charm hanging on a gold chain around her neck.

"I thought there were try-outs," I say.

"Yeah, but we have the coach on our side. Since we're the best players, if we want someone in, she's in." Crystal still doesn't look at me when she says this, but continues admiring Marissa's outfit, checking out the label inside the back of her shirt.

"Hey, who wants a ciggi butt?" Suzanne makes a "V" with her fingers and sucks air through them. "I'm dying for one."

"Me, too," Crystal says. "I'll beat you to the woods." She turns around and runs toward a wooded area next to the Teen Center. Suzanne and Marissa sprint after her. I try to catch up.

15

When I reach the woods, the three girls are sitting on stumps in a small clearing. Suzanne exhales a thin stream of smoke like they do in the movies. I'm sure she's been practicing in front of the mirror. She hands her cigarette to Marissa, who uses it to light hers. Crystal is holding a book of matches with fancy writing on it, probably from an expensive restaurant. She strikes a match, but the wind blows it out. Then she cups her hand around the second match and lights her cigarette.

"You have to join the lacrosse team, Marissa," Suzanne says.

"But my father is such a soccer fanatic. He was like Varsity, All-State, you name it." She blows a big puff of smoke out of her mouth. She hasn't gotten down the cool way of smoking. I hope she never does.

"Why do you listen to your father? I never listen to mine." Crystal looks up at the stars as if they are the only ones who can tell her what to do.

"It's different with you," Marissa says.

"Why?" Crystal asks, examining the bottom of her hair for split ends.

"Well, you know, 'cause your father isn't at home. It's a lot easier not to listen to him when you only see him once a week when he takes you out for dinner."

"I wouldn't listen to him if he lived at home. I don't listen to my mother and she lives at home. She's always giving me grief about smoking in my room."

"You smoke at home?" I ask. I can't imagine that.

"Allie could never do that," Marissa says. "Her mother is really anti-smoking."

"Really?" Suzanne asks. "Does she like check your breath when you get home and stuff? That's why mints were invented." She pops one in her mouth.

"No, but she used to smoke, so now every time she reads an article about lung cancer, she thinks she's going to die." I look for a stump to sit on, but there aren't any more, so I lean up against a tree. I feel stupid being kind of far away from the group.

"She sounds mental." Crystal throws down her cigarette butt, and grinds it into the dirt with the pointy toe of her shoe.

"Well, no." I look at Marissa for support. She always said my mother was one of the cooler moms. But Marissa stands up and starts swaying to the music. "I don't really like the taste of smoke anyway," I say.

"I'll bet she's never even tried it," Crystal snaps, looking at Marissa to see if this is true. Marissa shrugs. She's acting like she doesn't know me.

"Hey," Suzanne says, "let's go. I want to see if Sam Neufield is there. He kind of hinted he might make it." She takes a brush out of her handbag and starts brushing her ponytail.

"He is major cute," Marissa says. "He's in my English class this year and everyone has a crush on him." Crystal stands up and starts bopping to the music next to Marissa, mimicking her dance moves.

"Well, he's mine tonight. He was IM-ing me all last night. He said he loves girls who play lacrosse, and I'm totally into boys who play lacrosse." She flips her ponytail back off her face like a restless racehorse.

"Is he ever without that lacrosse stick?" I ask, but no one answers me. I know they heard me. My stomach is beginning to hurt. I wish I was at home.

"I'm going to be so all over Sam's best friend, Josh Bryce," Crystal says in a throaty, trying-to-be-sexy voice.

"Josh's been at your locker all week," Marissa says. "Every time I came to see you, there he was."

Crystal laughs her shrill laugh. "He made me promise I would go to his next lacrosse game. As if I would miss it."

"He's in love." Suzanne starts dancing with the other two.

I feel funny standing so far away, so I inch closer to them. "Yeah," I say. "It definitely sounds like he likes you."

Crystal suddenly stops dancing. Looking straight at Marissa and Suzanne, she says, "You know something, I think there's a tick here."

"What do you mean?" shrieks Suzanne. "Like a lyme-disease-type tick?" She starts checking her arms and legs. "People can die from that disease or lose control of their legs and stuff."

"No, I mean a leech-type person. Someone who gloms onto you like a bloodsucker and you can't get rid of her." Crystal stares right at me, her eyes narrow slits.

I look at Marissa to see what she'll say. She's biting her thumbnail. "Let's just go. All the good music will be over if we don't go in right now." Marissa takes Crystal's arm.

"Sure," Crystal says. "Only I don't want to take the tick with us. I don't want her sticking to us all night."

"I don't really think..." Suzanne is half-smiling like she doesn't know whether Crystal is kidding or not.

"Marissa," I say. "Maybe we'd better go home. My mother is supposed to pick us up at ten-thirty, but I can call her, and she can come sooner." The smell of cigarette smoke is making me sick.

"No, Marissa's not going home with you, Tick. She told us she had to bring you along tonight. She'll be glad if we get rid of you for her." Crystal holds up her book of matches. "My father told me he used to burn ticks with a match. He'd watch them shrivel up and die."

"Crystal, we'd better..." Marissa is beginning to look scared.

Crystal lights a match. "Burn, Tick, Burn," she chants. She throws the lit match at me. "Go find someone else to leech onto." She steps closer to me. The light-colored liquid make-up on her face makes her look like a ghost. She lights another match and throws it at me. "Burn, Tick!" she yells. The smell of sulfur burns my nostrils.

"Leave me alone," I say, backing up. She lights another match and before she can throw it, I fall over a branch and land hard on my butt.

Crystal stands over me. She holds the lit match close to my hair. "Burn," she whispers.

"Come on, Crystal, let's go inside so we can dance." Marissa moves towards us. "It's getting cold out here."

"I want to go home." My face is warm. I can't breathe. I feel like I'm choking. "I just want to go home. Let's go, Marissa." Tears start pouring down my face.

Crystal leans in closer. "Then go home. Just stay away from us, you big Tick." It sounds like she's really far away. Like I'm in a dream and her words are ringing in my ears. Suddenly my head feels hot and I can smell something burning.

"Oh my God!" Marissa yells. "You burned her hair!" She bats at my head with her sweatshirt.

"Is it out?" Suzanne steps towards us, but slowly as if she's afraid her hair will catch on fire, too. Everyone seems to be moving in slow motion and when they talk, it sounds like echoes.

"Yeah, but some of it got burned. It really smells. You okay?" Marissa asks me.

I reach for the back of my head. The ends of my hair feel singed like dry seaweed. A clump of my frizzy red hair falls off in my hands.

"Let's get out of here," Crystal crams the matches and her cigarettes into her pocketbook as if she's hiding the evidence.

"We can't just leave her." Marissa takes the shreds of hair from my hand and shows them to Crystal.

Crystal grabs my hair and throws it into the stream. "It's just hair. It'll grow back. Now come on. We don't want to be caught back here." She grabs Marissa's arm and drags her away.

"Yeah," Suzanne says. "Crystal and I are already on probation at the Teen Center. They told us that if they catch us back in these woods again, we'll be banned from coming to dances."

"All right. Let's go," Crystal says. "And if anyone asks, we have no idea where Allie is." She gives me a distant stare as if I already don't exist.

"But…" Marissa says, guiltily looking at me.

"And if she knows what's good for her, she won't go blabbing about this to anyone," Crystal says. "We can make her life miserable at school."

Suzanne grabs her bag and quickly follows Crystal, who drags Marissa by the arm. Then the three of them run away along the path to the Teen Center. I hear the sound of their feet on dry leaves as I grasp my hands around my neck and bend over, trying to curl my body into as small a shape as possible.

16

"*H*ush," Dorothy May whispers into my ear. I'm hunched over, sitting on a damp tree stump. I've been crying so hard my eyelids sting and my legs are starting to cramp from sitting in one place for so long. I'm not sure if it was the stream running through the woods or my watery tears that attracted Dorothy here.

It's gotten darker since Marissa, Crystal, and Suzanne left me, though moonlight filters through the trees, lighting up Dorothy's face. It's such a kind face with her round eyes and shy smile. I wonder if that's the first thing William Bradford noticed about her.

"*I pray thee leave this place. Surely there be wolves about these woods.*" Dorothy looks much more comfortable now that she's changed into the velvet gown and the Snow White slippers I gave her. She kneels down next to the stream and dips the end of the long gown into it. Then she wrings it out and wipes my eyes with the cool, wet cloth.

Soon I begin to feel better, but really tired. Crying is exhausting. No wonder babies are always sleeping. I can hear crickets chirping in the woods, and farther away, kids outside the Teen Center laughing and talking.

Some boys are singing along to the song "Y.M.C.A." I picture them forming the letters with their bodies. Boys in eighth grade have a lot more fun than girls. They don't care so much what other people think. They're allowed to be goofy. I wish I could join them and point my arms to the sky to create a "Y" with my body.

Dorothy strokes my head in a soothing way, but suddenly she cries out, *"Heavens! What happened to thy hair? Did someone accuse thee of being a witch and try to burn thee?"*

I quickly cover the back of my hair with my hand. "No, they don't burn witches at the stake anymore. A girl threw a match at me."

"Good Mistress Marissa?"

"No, her name is Crystal."

Dorothy abruptly stands up and crosses her arms. *"Thou must go home upon this instant."*

I look up at her pleadingly. "But if I call my mother now, she'll ask all these questions to find out why I'm leaving early. She's pretty good at figuring out if stuff is wrong. She's a psychologist."

"Psy-chol-o-gist? 'Tis an unfamiliar word. Does thy mother predict the future like a fortune teller?"

"My mother works in my school, so if kids have problems—like they're flunking out and they need to talk—they go see her."

"Must be mighty weak children to burden thy mother with their troubles." She shakes her head in disgust.

"No, sometimes kids really need someone to talk to. You know, maybe if you had someone to talk to, you wouldn't have jumped off the Mayflower." I blurt this out before I realize what I'm saying.

"Art thou as well a psy-chol-o-gist? Canst thou see into my soul?" She picks up a stone and wildly throws it into the stream. It bounces off a boulder and lands in the water with a huge splash.

"No, but I'm a psychologist's daughter. Some of it probably rubbed off on me." I walk over to her and try to take her hand, but she pulls it away.

"Then I will tell thee this, psy-chol-o-gist's daughter. Tonight thou became acquainted with terror." She spits this out like she's angry with me.

"Yes. It was horrible. I can't stop thinking about it. I was so scared." I shiver as I remember it.

"Then remember well that terror and put thyself in my shoes. For nigh on many months, the sailors told us terrible tales of the New World. 'Here is where wild beasts and savage men tear people limb from limb,' were their words. The moment I set eyes upon the shore, I could see nothing but darkness. Not a house. Not a light. Only miles of frightening forest. The darkness and chill winds rattled my soul so, I could scarce keep my wits about me."

A chill goes up my spine as I imagine how frightened Dorothy must have been as she faced her new life in a strange wilderness.

Dorothy looks off into the woods as if seeing something there.

"You don't need to be scared now," I say. "Nothing is going to hurt you." I can still hear the boys from the Teen Center singing. "Those aren't savages. Only eighth-grade boys."

Dorothy walks to a tree and inspects a yellowing leaf. *"Alas, the leaves change to the color of autumn. Summer comes to an end. 'Twas summer when last I saw my wee boy."* When she turns to face me, her eyes are so dark with sadness, I'm afraid if I touch her she'll collapse. She tosses the leaf into the stream and it rides the current toward the Teen Center.

"Do you know what happened to your son?" I ask.

"I have nary a word of him. The Saints forbade my seeing him." Her eyes flash angrily.

"Who are the Saints?"

"'Tis the name the Separatist Mayflower passengers bestowed upon ourselves. 'Twas thought we were God's chosen people and would receive eternal life in the hereafter."

"Then you did receive eternal life. I mean, you're still alive, or something," I say.

"If thou canst call this life. To walk the earth in search of mine only child," she cries out.

"But why won't they let you see him?" I ask.

"'Tis a formidable sin to kill thyself in my religion. Even in death, they shun me." She clenches her teeth to keep her lips from trembling as she tries not to cry.

"So in heaven, or wherever you come from, you haven't seen your son all these years?"

"Nay. Not since he was a child. William and I were allotted one wooden chest for which to pack all our worldly possessions. But the most valuable, I had to leave behind." She hugs her arms around her body as if it aches from emptiness.

"How terrible." I take Dorothy's hand and seat her on a stump. Tears fall from her eyes till her face becomes splotched with red spots. I dip the end of my t-shirt into the stream and kneel down beside her to wipe her face. I shiver from a sudden gust of wind.

"Ah, thou art cold." She tugs on the bottom of my chopped-off t-shirt. *"Thy garment does not cover much of thee. Surely someone will come to retrieve thee."*

"But I don't want them to know that Marissa left me here to go with her creepy new friends." I dig a hole with my toe and place the matches inside. Crystal's words echo in my ear, "Tick, tick, tick." Maybe I should bury myself in the dirt, too.

"Wouldst thou agree 'tis time to make new friends?"

"How can I? Everyone makes their friends in kindergarten, and that's your group for the rest of the time you're in school."

"But it seems Good Mistress Marissa has new friends, 'creepy' as they may be."

"Marissa can make new friends because she's beautiful and outgoing."

"Art thou not considered beautiful?"

"Me? Never. Not unless being beautiful is having bushy, red hair, mud-colored eyes, and King-Kong-size feet."

"In our congregation, 'twas taught to care more about the soul of a person than thy appearance."

"Doesn't work that way in middle school."

"Thou shalt see. What life has to bring thee, is still in the future." She pats me on the back. *"Canst thou send a message to thy mother so that she might convey thee home?"*

"Yeah, I can call her." I yank out my purple cell phone from my handbag. I was so excited when my mother took me to buy it the year I started middle school, imagining all the friends I would call.

"*A most wondrous invention,*" Dorothy says as I start to punch numbers on my cell. The phone number I've had forever. The phone number my parents made into a song when I was little so I could memorize it and call them if I ever got lost.

"Will you stay with me until they get here?" I ask.

"*Aye. I shall.*" She looks me in the eye with her steady gaze. "*For as long as it shall take.*" I hear my mother's voice on the end of the line and take a deep breath before I speak.

17

Standing by the curb waiting for my mother, I can't believe the stupid dance is already over. Kids are starting to pour out of the Teen Center. Where is she? There's not even a place to hide. Some moron cut down all the trees in front of the Teen Center so kids couldn't hang out and smoke pot in them. But they forgot about the woods next to it, which is now everyone's favorite place for drinking and smoking.

I spot a yellow baseball cap on the ground that someone must have lost. It has the words "Bee Nice" written in script with embroidered bees buzzing around on it. How corny. On my cell phone, I dial Mom's number again.

"Where are you?" I ask when Mom answers.

"Right in front of you." She pulls up in the red station wagon she calls her "red-hot-mama car," rolls down the window, and says, "Hop in, Kiddo."

I snatch the "Bee Nice" cap from the ground and shove it on my head as I grab the handle of the door to the back seat. I hope, she won't smell my burnt hair.

"Oh, no," she says. "Not in the back. My days of chauffeuring were over when we gave your car seat to Goodwill."

I jerk open the door on the passenger side and throw myself in. Instead of looking at my mother, I stare out the window.

"So, not having any fun, huh?" she asks. Under her raincoat, she's wearing her old pajamas, the ones with cats and dogs printed on them that Dad bought her years ago. "Well, it's probably better you're not a party girl. I wasted a lot of time in middle school socializing." She turns to look at me. "Hey, cute hat."

"Thanks," I say softly. I don't trust my voice. Mom's being so nice that I feel like crying and letting her hug me.

"So Marissa wanted to stay?"

I nod. I pray that Marissa doesn't appear. Mom would try to convince her to get in the car to drive her home.

"Did they have any good snacks at least?"

"Yeah, they had like nachos and uh, lemonade." I don't want her to know I never even made it inside. "Can we go now?"

"What's your rush? It's just boring old Daddy and me at home. Will's at Alex's house practicing with his band." She leans her head out the window. "Hey, listen to that song. I love Blondie." Mom starts singing, tapping her fingers on the steering wheel. She gazes out at the kids swaying to the music. "You know, Allie, you should dance while you're young; you don't get that many chances when you get older." Mom glances at herself in the rear-view mirror and sadly touches a grey streak in her hair.

"It's not so great to be young." I hear Crystal's high-pitched giggle and see a bunch of guys gathered around her, Marissa, and Suzanne.

"Why? Did something happen tonight, Allie?" Her voice gets soft and concerned.

"No."

"Did something happen with Marissa?"

"No."

"Because I have to say, I was surprised you were going out with her tonight. She hasn't been around much lately."

"Nothing's wrong."

"Well, I hope you'll tell me if something happened between you two. Believe it or not, I can remember how friends fight, and I see it every day at school."

"I don't need counseling."

"I didn't say you did. But you know if there's…"

"Mom, you're blocking traffic." Some kids are staring at our car probably trying to figure out who the idiots are that are taking so long to leave. Large raindrops begin falling on the roof of the car. My mother presses the window button to close it. Kids scramble toward the cars or dash back inside.

"Look," Mom says. "There's Marissa. She might need a ride." She presses the window button again and it begins to roll back down.

"Close the window!" I yell.

"Allie, what's the matter with you? Marissa's getting soaked." She looks at me as if I'd gone crazy.

"I don't care! Please, Mom, please. We have to get out of here."

"But we can't just leave Marissa here."

She tries to open the window again, but I scream, "No! You don't understand. I never want to see Marissa again." My voice is shaking and I feel dizzy.

"Please tell me what happened, Allie." She pulls up the brim of the baseball cap so she can see my eyes. I quickly push it back down. "Your eyes are red. You've been crying." She sounds scared.

I try to stop the tears, but a few roll down my face. I wish I could talk to her about the night so she'll hug me and tell me everything will be all right.

"I can't tell you." I lean my head back against the head-rest. "I just can't." My mother finally starts the engine and pulls away from the curb. As I look out the window, I see Marissa standing in the rain by herself, her perfect outfit soaked.

My mother asks, "What's that smell? Like something burnt." And I collapse into tears.

18

When we reach home, I jump out of the car and run into the house. I try to sneak past my father who is sitting in his recliner in the family room doing a crossword puzzle. I always tell him I can't see the fun in them. It's like the worst part of school—the homework.

"Hey, princess," he calls out. "You're not getting by me without paying the toll." This is an old game from when I was little.

"I'm too tired." I walk toward the stairs. "Good night, Dad."

"No you don't, missy. You're not dissing your old man." He's wearing another of his favorite t-shirts. This one reads, "I'm Old, Fat, and Happy About It."

"I'm not 'dissing' you. I just want to go to bed," I say. Mom comes in behind me. She looks kind of nervous, as if she doesn't know what to say to me, which is unusual. She always seems to have the answers.

"Come on, Allie, give your father a good-night kiss, and let's get you into the bathtub." My mother starts making neat piles of the magazines on the coffee table. This is weird. She hardly ever straightens up.

"She's going to take a bath at eleven o'clock?" my father asks. "I guess you must have gotten awfully sweaty dancing with those hunky eighth graders."

"Right." I kiss my father quickly on the cheek. He grabs me and, as he gives me a big hug, I smell the familiar scent of his shaving cream. "I can't believe my little girl is old enough to go to a dance. Why I remember when you were no bigger than my thumb." He wiggles his thumb like it's dancing.

"Good night, Dad." I start to leave, but he holds onto my arm.

"Allie, were there people smoking at the dance?" He takes a big sniff of me. "You smell like smoke."

"No, I don't." I try to pull away.

"You'd better not have been smoking, Allie. You want your mother to pull out the statistics on smokers?"

"Let's save the anti-smoking campaign for another day, Doug," she says.

"Fine, it's your soap box. I was just trying to help." He looks down at his newspaper as if he'll find the answer to my mother's confusing behavior in the crossword puzzle.

"I think she's had a bad night." My mother leads me to the couch and gently sits me down.

"I'm so cold," I say. My mother takes the blanket from the back of the couch and wraps it around me, taking a seat next to me.

"I'm sorry you had a bad night." My father rises from his chair and sits on my other side. They both put their arms around me and I snuggle into them.

"Remember, we're always here for you, Allie." My mother kisses my cheek.

My father starts massaging my shoulders. "What's that smell?" he asks. I quickly grab hold of my baseball cap with both hands, but Dad snatches it off my head.

"Oh my God!" my father shouts. "What happened to your hair?" And for what feels like the hundredth time tonight, I begin to cry.

19

In Mr. Sampson's class Monday morning, Marissa writes in her notebook probably so she doesn't have to look at me while I read from my journal. I've always hated how thick my red hair is, but today I'm thankful there's so much of it. When it's in a ponytail, you can't see the bald spot where it was burned.

⌦⫶⌫

Alice Toth
Class: English: Mr. Sampson

MAKING A NEW START

The Pilgrims first went to Holland to find religious freedom, but after they'd been there for a while, they started losing their English language and customs. For instance, their children didn't want to speak English anymore—they spoke Dutch. That's when the Pilgrims decided to come to America and make a new start.

It makes me wonder. Do people have to pack up everything and go on a dangerous voyage to find an uninhabited land, so that they can create the kind of life that is right for them? To find friends who think the same way they do and who they can get along with? I just don't think there are that many empty places in the world where people can run away to anymore if you don't get along with the people who live nearby to you.

Mr. Sampson smiles at me when I finish reading to the class. I'm so exhausted from a weekend of lying to my parents that I can barely keep my eyes open. The interrogation was pretty intense, with my father threatening to call the police to report the person who burned my hair.

My mother tried to worm it out of me with psychological tricks. "You should really tell us, Allie. What if this happened again? You could end up in the hospital."

I told them that I was standing next to someone who was smoking in the parking lot, but I don't think they believed me, especially when my brother said, "There's no way anyone could smoke within fifty feet of the Teen Center without getting busted." Thanks, Will. But I stuck to my story. The last thing I need is to get a reputation as a tattletale.

"What do you all think about what Allie has written?" Mr. Sampson asks, rubbing his buzz-cut. He tries to avoid Mathew Huddle's wildly waving hand, but gives in when no one else volunteers.

"I like what she says about how it's hard for people to get along with all our differences." His voice squeaks on the word "differences." He takes off his glasses and nervously wipes them with his shirt. "Sometimes I think no one likes me, either."

I almost choke.

"I don't think Allie was saying that no one liked her. She's a very likable girl." Mr. Sampson gives me a big old goofy wink.

"Well, my mother says that the popular kids never do well in life because they're so busy trying to stay popular they never have time to study." Mathew gives me a thumbs-up sign, like we're in this unpopular club together. I want to hide under my desk and have it collapse on top of me.

"An interesting theory, Mathew," Mr. Sampson says. "But I hate to tell you that sometimes popular kids do very well in life. As much as most of us would like to think otherwise."

"Hey, Mr. S.," Josh Bryce yells out. He has a big smile on his face so you can see his adorable chipped tooth, which he chipped last year playing lacrosse. "Were you popular?" Figures Josh would be the one to ask, since everyone likes him.

"I had my friends," Mr. Sampson says. "And that's all you really need. Just a couple of guys or girls to pal around with and help you out when you get in trouble. Even one person will do."

I sneak a look at Marissa, but I don't think she's listening. She's too busy ripping a page out of her notebook and folding it into a tiny square. Her highlighted hair falls over her face, hiding it.

"All right, I have an announcement," Mr. Sampson says. "Allie and her journal have inspired me to take you on a class trip."

"A Knicks' game! Yahoo!" Josh calls out.

"'Fraid not," Mr. Sampson says. "But almost as exciting. The administration has agreed to a field trip to Plimoth Plantation. You'll get to talk to actors who play the real Pilgrims."

"Did the Pilgrims play basketball?" Sam Neufield asks. Josh's best friend has shaggy-blonde hair to his shoulders like a lot of the lacrosse jocks. I can see why Suzanne might like him.

"Unfortunately not. The only sport you might see there is stool-ball. It's a game they played in the 1600's, where the players would hit the ball and then run between stools."

"Kind of like cricket," Josh says.

"Exactly. Someone knows his English sports." Mr. Sampson starts handing out permission slips. "Have these back to me by Friday. Plymouth is a couple hour bus ride from here."

After checking out his permission slip, Mathew Huddle squeaks. "Hey, Mr. Sampson. You spelled Plymouth wrong."

"That's how they spell Plimoth Plantation. It is ye olde way of spelling Plymouth; P-l-i-m-o-t-h," Mr. Sampson replies. "Okay, who's next with his or her journal project? No volunteers? All right. Here goes." Mr. Sampson closes his eyes and, with his arm extended, he spins.

That's when I notice the folded note on my desk and see Marissa motioning for me to open it. Maybe Marissa has been listening to Mr. Sampson talk about friendship, and she's ready to be friends again. She realizes that all you need in life is one good friend. And, of course, I'll forgive her for the other night. After all, she was trying to help me, and would have, if the evil Crystal hadn't been there.

Mr. Sampson stops and opens his eyes, his arm out-stretched. I hide the note in my notebook so he can't see it. "Marissa?" he asks, but she shakes her head. "Come on, you're not keeping up with your journal project," he says. Marissa looks out the window. I can tell Mr. Sampson is disappointed. He puts his hand over his eyes and begins to spin again.

While he's spinning, I quickly open the note. And there in Marissa's precise script, signed Marissa, with a heart over the "i" like she always does, she has written the words, "You better not have told anyone about what happened the other night." I wonder if anyone can hear my heart breaking.

20

At the end of class, I slowly pick up the Dorothy May journal and slide it into my backpack between the earth science and math books. I can't believe Marissa doesn't care that Crystal burned my hair. Does she really hate me that much? Everything has changed so much since this summer, when we spent every afternoon in my pool talking about how great eighth grade was going to be.

Sara Borden stops by my desk. I don't know her very well. She moved to our town last year and mostly keeps to herself. "I liked what you wrote in your journal about finding friends who think the same way you do. It's kind of hard, isn't it?" she asks.

"Yeah, it is," I say. I catch Marissa's glance, see her perfectly-tweezed eyebrows raised, like she's really giving up on me if I'm talking to Sara Borden. Marissa makes fun of the artsy way Sara dresses. Today she's wearing a head-band in her stick-straight brown hair. She must have made it by braiding together those long skinny balloons, which are used for making balloon animals. I can hear Marissa in my head saying, "Why doesn't she just do everybody a favor and pick up a copy of *Seventeen*?"

"I'm glad we're going to Plimoth Plantation. It should give me some interesting people to sketch." Sara taps her pencil on her sketchbook. Marissa is inching over, making me nervous.

"Do you think they'll have an actor playing Dorothy May there?" Sara asks.

"Probably not. She died before they started the colony." As Marissa gets closer, my stomach starts to feel queasy.

"Right. But she could be represented on the reproduction of the Mayflower."

"I guess." Out of the corner of my eye I see Marissa mouthing something to me. When I turn, I realize that what she's saying is, "Picasso wannabe." That's what she calls Sara because she's always drawing.

Sara turns and sees what Marissa is saying.

"Oh," she says to me. "I don't need this. Stupid childish games. I thought you were different." She tosses her beaded pocketbook over her shoulder and struts out the door.

"Wait," I say, but it's too late. Sara obviously thinks I agree with Marissa's insult of her. And maybe I would have in the past. But now I'm not so sure.

Marissa tosses her shiny blonde hair over her shoulder and gives me a triumphant look. "You should thank me for getting rid of that art freak for you." Before I can say anything, she bounces out of the room, probably to meet Crystal and tell her what a loser I am for talking to Sara.

Soon everyone has left the classroom except for Josh who's talking with Mr. Sampson at his desk. I overhear Josh saying,

"So I was thinking for the journal project I could write as if I was an alien from the planet Neptune or something. I could write stuff like, 'It's very cold here on Neptune. We only have icicles to eat. Send blankets.'" He grins at Mr. Sampson.

Mr. Sampson nods, but says, "I think you'd run out of things for your alien to say pretty quickly. Why don't you find something more personal to write about? That's where all good writing comes from. Something that really means something to the writer."

"But I am personally interested in aliens." Josh doodles on the cover of his notebook as if he's embarrassed.

Just as I'm just about to step out the door, Mr. Sampson calls out to me. "Hey, Allie, come here a minute."

I slowly walk over to them. Josh combs his fingers through his wavy, dark-brown hair and looks at me warily. I'm sure he thinks I'm a school-nerd like everyone else. I know he used to have a crush on Marissa, but then, all the boys have at one time or another.

"I want you to help Josh come up with an idea for his journal," Mr. Sampson says, putting his hand on Josh's shoulder.

"Really? But I don't know what to tell him." My face is feeling hot and I know it must be turning red. I cover my cheeks with my hands so Josh won't see.

"Yeah, how can Allie help me? She doesn't know anything about me." It seems like he's mad at me. This wasn't my dumb idea.

"I'm sure she'll be able to help you, Josh." Mr. Sampson starts sorting through some papers on his desk. "School isn't just about book learning, you know. It's about learning how to cooperate with other people. So, both of you start cooperating and come up with something for Josh's journal by tomorrow. Lacrosse may just have to wait, Josh."

Josh rushes out of the room while I trail after him. Stopping at the water fountain, he takes a long drink. I feel stupid waiting for him, but it would be rude to walk away. He stands up and wipes the water off his chin with the back of his hand. Some of it dribbles down his t-shirt. He stares down the hallway, probably to see if any of his friends are there. "So you got any ideas?" he asks.

"Not really." I look away. "I don't know why Mr. Sampson wants me to help you. I'm sure you'll do fine on your own."

"He doesn't think so. I guess he has something against aliens." He looks at me with this sad, poor-me look, and I can feel my face getting warm again.

"Do you have any other ideas?" I wonder if any girls in the hallway are watching me. They'd be very curious as to why Josh is talking to me. I can just hear them now, gossiping about Josh and me in the lunchroom. Too bad it's about some dumb school thing.

"Not really." He shifts his heavy backpack from one arm to the other as if it's light as air. There's a lacrosse patch sewn onto the front pocket.

"How did you come up with your idea?" He looks straight into my eyes and I wonder why I had never noticed that he has this blue spot in one of his hazel-colored eyes. How cool is that?

"My mother is totally obsessed with her ancestors and she told me the story of Dorothy May, even though she isn't really my ancestor."

The bell rings for the next class and I pause for Josh to dash down the hall, but he doesn't. "After Dorothy jumped off the Mayflower, my ancestor married her ex-husband. I was named after her. Alice." One of my red curls escapes from the ponytail and falls into my face. I brush it back.

"Oh, yeah. I was named after my great-grandfather." He grins like he's feeling a little more relaxed. I wish I could. I mean, he's just a person. Why do I feel so nervous?

"Do you know anything about him?" I ask, twirling the stray curl around my finger.

"Yeah, he was this country doctor and people would pay him by giving him cows and chickens and stuff. I've even got his old doctor's bag and pictures of him from medical school. I used to love hearing stories about him." Josh starts talking faster. He's obviously enjoying telling me about his great-grandfather.

"He sounds really neat." Oh, no. Did I just say "neat"? Josh is going to think I'm a total nerd now.

"Yeah, he was. Oh, and in our attic is this human skeleton that used to belong to him. Doctors in those days had their own skeletons, so they could figure out how the bones fit together." He takes my hand and bends one of my fingers as if demonstrating a skeleton's bones.

"Wow. I didn't know that." I am never washing that hand.

"We used to ask my mother if we could stick it out on the porch for Halloween, but she said it would be way too scary for little kids."

"For big kids, too." I think my face has finally settled into its normal color without a trace of embarrassed red. "Well, your great-grandfather sounds great. Maybe you could use him for your journal."

"You think so?"

"Sure."

"That might work. Because I want to be a doctor, too." He hesitates as he says this.

"Really? You want to be a doctor?"

"Why? You don't think I could do it?" He stares straight into my eyes as if what I say about his future actually matters.

"Sure you could. I just didn't know you wanted to be a doctor."

"I don't talk about it a lot. Well, you know, in case my grades aren't good enough. But ever since I heard about my great-grandfather, I've wanted to be a doctor." Is his face turning pink? I've never seen Josh embarrassed. He bends down to take another sip of water from the fountain, probably to give his face time to cool off. I can't believe I'm getting a glimpse of the human side of Josh Bryce—the part with real feelings.

"Well, I can't wait to hear your journal in class tomorrow."

"Yeah. I wish I didn't have lacrosse practice after school. I'm going to be up all night writing this thing."

"It shouldn't be that hard," I say. "You already know a lot about your great-grandfather. Maybe you should bring in the skeleton."

"You think that would get me an 'A?'" he asks, and smiles that great chipped-tooth smile.

"Sure." I smile back, trying not to open my mouth too wide because I know that makes me look silly. "It couldn't hurt." As I start to turn away, he calls after me, "Hey Allie! I bet you look like your ancestor, the one you're named after."

"You think so?"

"Yeah, she's probably the one you got your great red hair from." And as the last bell rings, he waves and jogs down the hall toward his class.

Great red hair, I think. Wow. And, as I gently touch my hair as if rewarding it for getting Josh's attention, I sense someone looking at me. I turn around to see that it's Crystal, who is standing across the hall in front of her locker, staring straight at me with an expression full of hate.

21

I hurry down the hall towards my class. I can't believe Josh likes my hair. And who would have guessed that his parents talk about their ancestors, too? I thought my parents were the only ones who discussed their dead relatives around the dinner table, the same way other families talk about friends who are still alive.

It's funny, but in a way, Dorothy May brought Josh and me together. If I hadn't met Dorothy May, then I wouldn't have written about her in my journal, and then Mr. Sampson wouldn't have thought of asking me to talk to Josh, and then I wouldn't have found out that he likes talking about his great-grandfather.

Dorothy May is so great. I wish there was something I could do to make her happy. She's a much better friend than Marissa, even though she's dead. I reach into the pocket of my skirt and pull out the note Marissa gave me and tear it into tiny pieces. I could have third-degree burns all over my body and all she'd care about was whether she and her dumb friends were going to get into trouble.

.Just then someone knocks into me, making me drop my backpack on the floor. "Move your butt," Crystal says. She flips her highlighted hair at me like it's a weapon.

I bend down to pick up my backpack and she shoves me again so I fall on top of it hard on my knees. It really hurts. I steady myself and try to get up, but Crystal stands over me.

"Leave Josh alone," she hisses, putting her tiny hands on her hips and jutting out her chin at me. She sneaks a look down the hall to make sure Josh isn't within earshot.

I stare up at her face with its perfectly-tweezed eyebrows and the tiny nose just like Marissa's. She wears so much make-up it looks like she has the plastic face of a doll.

I imagine myself jumping to my feet, sticking my face in hers, and saying, *"Don't you think that's his decision? It's not like I forced him to talk to me."* My voice will be so super calm—it will force her to back down.

But instead, I stutter, "Oh, okay."

"'Cause you heard me talking about him the other night at the Teen Center," she says. "You know I like him, and he likes me." She leans in so close to my face I can smell the perfumed lotions she's smeared all over her body.

Her eyes blink rapidly and she starts rubbing one of them until her mascara smudges and there's a black ring under one eye.

"Yeah, he likes you," I say, my voice high.

"As long as we have that straight." She throws her back-pack over her shoulder and turns away from me. I imagine myself tripping her and saying, *"You'd better go to the girls' room and wash your face. It looks like you have a black eye. I don't think Josh likes that look, do you?"*

But all I say is, "Bye, Crystal." And, instead of feeling happy about my first real conversation with Josh, I feel defeated, once again, by Crystal. I get slowly to my feet, listening to the flip flop of her shoes echoing down the hallway.

22

But I know that's not the end of Crystal. I sneak into Spanish class while Señora Fishbein is writing on the blackboard. Her thick fingers push hard on the chalk and a piece breaks off. Without turning around, she calls out to me, "Tu llegaste tarde, Alicia." I slink to my seat, open my Spanish textbook, and try to disappear behind it.

From the conversation, I gather that we're supposed to pretend we're students in Spain preparing for a hiking trip. We have to figure out how to say in Spanish, "I must pack a can of peas" and "Is this the way to the mountain?"

Crystal tiptoes up to the door of our classroom and taps her nose with her finger three times—her secret signal to Marissa, who jumps up and asks Señora Fishbein for a hall pass. I can just imagine the major meeting of the three of them that will occur in the girls' room.

In the old days, Marissa would have defended me against Crystal and Suzanne. She would have told Crystal to apologize to me for burning my hair. But inside my pocket, I feel the torn pieces of Marissa's note, and I realize that she doesn't care about being my friend anymore. Instead she'll proudly tell Crystal how she warned me not to tell anyone about what happened the other night.

But Crystal will be more worried that I was talking to her boyfriend, and she'll tell them they have to come up with a plan to get even with me. And they'll all nod and act tough, glancing at themselves in the mirror, thinking how pretty and skinny they all look together and how superior they are to me.

But underneath it all, I know they'll be a little scared. They'll be thinking about what would happen if I reported them to the principal. That they might get suspended from school, and then their perfect little worlds would tumble down. Just think, they might have more to worry about than which boy to have a crush on this week.

I suppose I should be worried about what further torture Crystal has in mind for me, but right now I've got bigger things to think about. Such as how to conjugate the Spanish verb for "to hike." I hike. She hikes. They hike.

I wish Crystal would take a hike.

23

I'm counting bus stops. Only three more stops 'til I reach home. I already have it planned out. I'm going to sneak past my mother to my room, close the door, collapse into bed and pull the covers over my head.

But when the bus reaches my house, Marissa's mother's car is in the driveway. She has a white convertible, which Marissa calls her "Miss Bud" car because Mrs. Donnelly once won a Miss Budweiser pageant and got to sit on top of a white car like this in a parade and wave to people. Will is outside dumping plastic bags into the garbage bin, probably the only time I've seen him out of the house and not attached to a computer keyboard.

"Hey, I hear you set your hair on fire," he yells at me. "Nice going. Were you smoking pot or cigarettes? Or something stronger?" His thick hair looks even blonder in the sun. How unfair is that? He inherited the nice blonde hair and I got stuck with red.

"Very funny." I try to ignore him and sneak into the side door without my mother and Mrs. Donnelly seeing me. What is she doing here? Did my mom call her and tell her about the other night?

"You can tell me, Allie," he says putting on a fake sincere look. "You know your secret will die with me." He shoves the lid on the garbage can and tries to smash down the over-flowing garbage. A couple of carrot stubs and a milk carton fall out, which he ignores.

"There's another can in the garage, you know. You don't have to try to squeeze it all into one," I say.

"Oh, yeah. Then go get it for me." Will smirks his weirdo smirk.

"Forget it," I say. "I am not your slave."

"Yes, you are," he says. "Or I'll tell Mom you're here, and you'll never be able to sneak up to your room."

"I don't care if she knows I'm here."

"Right." He crosses his arms and leans up against the garage door. "Do you know why Marissa's mom is here?"

"No, do you?"

"Yup, but it'll cost you."

I roll my eyes.

"Like I might give you something for nothing," he snorts.

"What do you want?" I ask.

"Finish taking out the garbage." He wipes his hands on his pants to get the garbage slime off.

"Like I want to get all stinky like you."

"All right," he says, then smirks even bigger than before. He opens the door and yells in, "MOM! Allie's here!"

"Thanks, Will," she calls out in that extra-sweet voice she uses when company's here. "Come here, Allie!"

And that's when I get this sinking feeling that I've been caught. And I didn't even do anything wrong.

Will puts his arm around me. "Sorry, Al. I know what it's like to be in trouble."

"Thanks." I shake my head. "I guess."

24

My mother and Mrs. Donnelly are in the family room. My mother sits cross-legged in a puffy, flowered chair wearing one of her boring navy-blue sweatsuits. Mrs. Donnelly manages to look glamorous despite the fact that she's crammed into a corner of the couch, which is jam-packed with antique pillows. She's wearing a sweater set in her signature color, what she calls cerulean. It's really light blue, but I guess if you used to be in the modeling business, you like to use fancy names for colors.

"So, Allie," she says, her precise way of speaking sounding even more formal than usual. "I understand there was a problem the other night with some fire." She emphasizes the word "fire" harshly like it could burn you.

"Yes," I say, "but I'm okay now. It was nice seeing you, Mrs. Donnelly. I have to go finish a project for uh…health class." Oh, why did I say health? They'll know I hardly ever have homework for health. I start to leave, but my mother stops me.

"Allie, I invited Diana here because I thought she should know that your hair was burned on the night you and Marissa went to the dance." She's using her calm psychologist voice, the one that always unravels me and makes me tell her whatever she wants to know. But it's not going to work this time.

"It was just an accident." I stand facing them, my legs are stiff, my back straight, and my hands are clasped behind me like I'm facing a firing squad. "I was next to someone who was playing with matches and my hair caught on fire."

"You told me someone was smoking next to you," my mother says.

"Well, it couldn't have been Marissa," Mrs. Donnelly cuts in. "She knows my feeling about those horrible wrinkle-causing sticks." She crinkles her nose in disgust.

"As Allie knows, I am thoroughly anti-smoking." My mother speaks slowly like she does when she's trying not to act mad. "But this is something bigger. I suspect that someone put a lit match to Allie's hair and..."

"You can't be saying that Marissa would do something so vile, Pam." Mrs. Donnelly picks up one of the antique pillows as if she wants to throw it at Mom.

"No, I'm only suggesting that Marissa and her new friends were there. They might know what happened," my mother says.

"I already told you what happened." My voice squeaks like Mathew Huddle's.

"And I think you're protecting someone," my mother says.

"If Marissa knew something, she would have told me. She tells me everything." Mrs. Donnelly says this proudly as if she and Marissa should get a prize for being the closest mother-daughter team in America.

"It's been my experience that when girls reach a certain age, even if they've been very close with their mothers, they stop revealing quite so much." My mother looks at me as she says this; I get her point.

"Okay, Pam, I know you have the Ph.D. in psychology and I don't..."

"I'm not saying..."

"Yes you are. You're the expert on kids. But I'm the expert on my daughter. I know her better than anyone, even you." The corners of Mrs. Donnelly's mouth twitch into a frown.

"I'm not blaming Marissa," my mother says, her voice getting louder. I can tell she's really mad. "I don't trust her new friends. Their names are on the mean-girl list of eighth-grade girls."

"There's a mean-girl list?" Mrs. Donnelly's voice hits high C.

"Well, not officially," my mother stutters, her face turning bright red. You can tell she accidentally let out some big school secret. "I didn't mean to say that. And Diana, please don't tell Marissa anything about this. Okay?"

Mrs. Donnelly nods, but I'll bet she's crossing her fingers behind her back like I do. "Marissa's name isn't on it, is it?" She brings the tips of her fingers together as if she's praying. In her modeling portfolio, which Marissa used to drag out, I remember Mrs. Donnelly posing like that in an advertisement for diamonds.

"No," my mother says. "And I want to make sure she stays off it. You know how much I care about Marissa after all these years, though I haven't seen her much lately."

Mrs. Donnelly's eyes open wide, the tips of her fake eyelashes touching her eyebrows. "What do you mean? She's here practically every day."

"She hasn't been here for at least two months," my mother says.

"But she told me..." Mrs. Donnelly sinks back into the couch and folds her arms over her chest. She crosses one leg over the other and her foot starts jerking up and down as if she wants to kick my mother.

Mrs. Donnelly turns her gaze to me. "Do you know where she's been going, Allie?" she asks in a strict-teacher voice as if it's me who's been hiding something from her, not Marissa.

"Not really." I keep my eyes on the floor. Oh, why did my mother have to drag Mrs. Donnelly into this? And why do I feel guilty?

My mother steps towards me and takes my hand. "Allie, this is important. If you know where Marissa has been going after school, you should tell us." She touches my hair, pulling a long piece over the part where she cut out the burned hair.

"Marissa's mentioned a girl named Crystal. Has she been going somewhere with her?" Mrs. Donnelly clutches her cerulean sweater around her as if she's cold.

"How am I supposed to know what Marissa does with her new friends?" I should just tell them what happened and get it over with. It's not like Marissa would lie for me.

"Allie, I want you to tell me right now where she's been going. I don't like to be lied to." Mrs. Donnelly whacks her hand on the arm of the sofa for emphasis while curling her lips into a grimace that sure wouldn't be found in any of her modeling photos.

I stare out the window, longing for someone to rescue me from Mrs. Donnelly.

"So you're not going to help me, Allie, after all I've done for you over the years?" Usually, Mrs. Donnelly is pretty nice, but now she's acting like she hates me. I know it's because she doesn't want to hear bad things about Marissa.

"Now, Diana, this isn't going to get us anywhere." My mother won't even look at Mrs. Donnelly.

"You're right. I'm not going to learn anything more about my daughter. I'm going home." Mrs. Donnelly pushes herself off the couch and grabs her brand-new handbag off the coffee table.

"Allie, Mrs. Donnelly just wants to make sure Marissa's not getting into trouble." My mother moves toward the door as if trying to block Mrs. Donnelly's exit.

"I don't know what you mean by trouble." I try to avoid looking at Mrs. Donnelly.

"Oh, come on, Allie," my mother says. "Do you think these girls might be the wrong friends for Marissa?"

I want to shout, *"Of course they're the wrong friends for Marissa! They shoplift and smoke cigarettes and they'll probably get Marissa to start drinking and flunk out of school along with them because they're so stupid and don't care about their grades!"*

But that would go against the kid code of honor. So I lie to my mother and Mrs. Donnelly. I say, "No, Marissa's friends are fine. They're really nice girls. I'm just not one of them." To my horror and embarrassment, my voice cracks.

Mrs. Donnelly says, "You poor dear."

I turn around, and run out of the room.

25

Even though Marissa and I aren't friends anymore, I decide I'd better warn her about her mother. I don't want her blaming me that I didn't tell her what was up.

I open my laptop and an Instant Message pops up. It says, "DIE allie DIE. U dont deserve 2 live."

Another IM pops up on my screen. "josh HATES red hair. he calls you that NERD." Then I notice the screen name. It's "crystal.lite."

The last one says, "crystal.lite: stay away from my BF if you know what's GFY."

Not that I would have answered Crystal, but before my fingers even touch the keys, a message says, "crystal.lite has logged off." Her messages scare me. I remember hearing about this girl who was interested in a boy that Crystal liked. Crystal took a picture of this girl changing in the locker room with her camera phone and posted it on the Internet.

Marissa's on Instant Messenger. We used to IM all the time. It feels funny to see her user name and not have a million things to say to her. Although I do have to tell her what happened with her mom.

allieoop: your mom came over today. knows u haven't been here 4ever. i didnt tell.

rissa: what about yr hair? does she know?

allieoop: mom spilled the beans.

rissa: great. i'll be grounded.

allieoop: not my fault. blame yr serial-killer friend.

rissa: betr watch what u say.

allieoop: crystal wants to kill me 4 talking 2 josh.

rissa: she's possessive. betr not talk 2 him anymore.

allieoop: last i checked it was a free country.

rissa: crystal liked him first. says theyre hangin out.

allieoop: remembr when crystal called us geeks in lunch-room last year. said what's on geek menu today?

rissa: i'm off her geek list since i got my braces off & guys ask her about me.

allieoop: GFU

rissa: what?

allieoop: good for u.

rissa: sarcasm, als?

allieoop: you expect me to be ☺ u dumped me?

rissa: didn't dump u.

allieoop: right. wait till crystal dumps u.

rissa: she won't.

allieoop: will too.

rissa: o, now yr psychic?

allieoop: nope. i just know.

rissa: yr weird.

allieoop. am not.

rissa: r 2. talk to a dead person in yr journal.

allieoop: I dont talk to her. its just an assignment.

rissa: but you think shes real.

allieoop: do not.

rissa: yr getting weirder & weirder.

allieoop: and yr getting meaner & meaner.

rissa: i just tell the truth. u need 2 straighten yr hair and get bettr clothes.

allieoop: i hate u.

rissa: whatever. crystal's IMing me. gotta go.

allieoop: tell her 2 stop threatening me.

rissa: tell your mom 2 stop talking to my mom.

allieoop: i cant control my mom.

rissa: i cant control crystal.

And the screen says, "rissa has logged off."

26

I open my math book and stare at the equations, but the numbers start flying around in my head so that nothing adds up. I glance at the photo on my bulletin board from last summer of Marissa and me swimming in the pool.

I feel someone behind me, and when I turn around, Dorothy May is leaning over my shoulder. Wisps of her brown hair frame her face and a piece of the ribbon I tied in her hair falls free. She looks much more relaxed and prettier.

"Canst thou let her go?" She points to Marissa in the photo.

"I can try." From my pocket, I remove the pieces of the note Marissa sent me in class. I open the window and one by one, I let go of each tiny piece, watching it fly away in the breeze.

"Ah. Is that an instrument?" Dorothy asks pointing to the open laptop on my desk. *"If it be so, perchance thou canst play a lovely song—a farewell to Marissa."*

"No, it's a computer. I use these letters to write with." I point to the keyboard.

She lightly touches the keys as if she's afraid of them. *"I could write but a few words. In truth, only my name."*

"You can only write your name?" I ask.

"Aye and I was most proud of that. 'Tis an accomplishment for a girl. If thou hast a quill, I will show thee."

"They don't use quills for writing anymore."

"'Tis a pity. My name looked most grand in letters. Mistress Dorothy May Bradford." As she draws the letters in the air, her mouth breaks into a proud smile.

I type her name. "Here you go," I say. "Mistress Dorothy May Bradford in a font called French Script."

She peers at her name on the screen. *"Oh wonders. Canst thou write anything thou likest?"*

"Sure, I write all the time. I know lots of words and if I spell them wrong, Spell-Check will fix them for me. See." I type "Mayfower" and the computer corrects it to "Mayflower."

Dorothy May claps her hands together. *"With this instrument, perchance we could write a letter to my son."* Her face shines with joy.

"Maybe." I don't have the heart to tell her that we couldn't contact a ghost from the seventeenth century because, for one thing, he definitely wouldn't have an e-mail address.

"And perhaps to have correspondence with my husband William," she says.

"Dorothy, do you think you could let William go if you found out what happened to him?"

"I believe so." She rubs her hands together as if comforting herself.

"Were you very much in love with him?"

"Aye, as a good wife should, I worshipped him, but he..." Her voice cracks. *"He broke my heart the night ...the night..."*

I take her hand and lead her gently to sit on the edge of my bed. "What happened on that night?" I ask quietly. "You must have felt so alone."

Her hands flutter restlessly until I stop them by holding onto them very tightly. She takes a very deep breath. *"It was a most wretched night. As the cold rains fell, the winds blew most harsh. William and sundry menfolk were launching a small boat, what we called a shallop, upon the seas to search for our new homeland. I begged William not to leave me, I was so afeared. With anger in his eyes, he tore my hands from around his neck and said, 'Why did the Good Lord see fit to bind me to a weakling such as thee? My beloved Alice has one-hundred times thy strength. She should be the one standing by my side on the deck of this sacred boat.'"*

"What a horrible thing to say," I cry out.

"Aye, I was pierced to my very being." She holds her hand over her heart and presses her lips together to keep from crying. *"I watched William upon the shallop fade into the distance, and I knew beyond doubt what fate lay before me—a most lonely life in a cold wilderness with a husband who did not love me, nor my son to comfort me."* A sob bursts forth from her.

I gently rub her back until the sobs subside and she weeps softly. "I wish there was something I could do to help you," I say.

"There is nothing to be done now." She stares sadly out the window, her face moist with tears. I grab a tissue from my nightstand and hand it to her. *"I am certain William fared better without me."*

"That's not true. He would have been happy with you if only he had given you a chance."

"Canst thou tell me if he was to marry again?" she asks.

I turn away, but she pulls me back. *"Please tell me. I can better lay to rest my feelings if I know."*

"He married Alice Carpenter."

"Oh!" she cries out and falls to the floor. I grab her by her arms and pull her onto my desk chair. *"My fears were realized,"* she sobs, her head falling into her hands.

"I'm afraid so."

"It should not matter now. Oh, why should I still feel this pain?" she shouts. *"When did they marry? Was I but newly in my watery grave?"*

"No," I say. "It was many years later after her first husband died. She came over to America." This is a little white lie, but it would be too painful for her if she knew that Alice came over on practically the next boat.

"I should have known they would marry. It was their fate." She folds her hands in her lap and looks almost calm now.

"And mine," I say quietly.

"Thy fate?" She looks puzzled at first, but then sinks into the chair almost in relief.

"Now I see why the spirits have united us. I was blind that I did not see before. Thou art kin to Alice Carpenter. Thou hast her hair, her coloring." She weaves a section of my hair between her fingers.

"Don't hate me. I know it sounds silly now, because we've become…friends. But when you first came, I was afraid that you'd put a spell on me if you found out." I try to pull away a little.

"If 'twere possible for me to cast spells, do you not think I would place one upon my husband to make him love me?"

"I hadn't thought of that." I smile in relief and she does as well. We sit silently for a moment while she makes tiny braids with my hair, wrapping the ends with ribbon, which she pulls from her own hair.

"If I were to have a daughter, I would like her to be like thee."

"Really?"

"Yes, thou hast been most kind."

"And you've been great to me." I wrap my arms around Dorothy and give her a big hug. Surprised, she steps back. I guess hugging wasn't a custom among the Pilgrims. But then she throws her arms around me and hugs me back with a powerful strength I didn't know she possessed.

"My son. Perchance you can tell me what happened to my son." She looks at me with such hope as the light from the sunset streams into her eyes from the window.

"Oh, I can tell you that," I say, happy to be able to provide her with the information she most craves. I open the binder labeled "Our Pilgrim Ancestors" and turn to the William Bradford page. "There's your son." I point to a line of type that said "John Bradford."

"Oh wonders." A great smile comes over her face.

"It says that your son came to America to live with his father in Plymouth. He lived until 1676. He was fifty-eight."

"Did he marry?" Dorothy May asks.

"Let me see." I take a deep breath and read, "John Bradford, son of William Bradford and Dorothy May Bradford, married in 1650 to Martha Bourne."

Dorothy May delicately touches the lines I've just read with the tips of her fingers. *"Martha Bourne,"* she says. *"A lovely name."*

"I'll bet you would have liked her." I hand the binder over to her.

She hugs the binder to herself and says, *"Yes. I know I would have liked Martha Bourne."*

27

When I walk into English class the next day, Josh is talking to Mr. Sampson in front of the classroom. Next to them, covered in the kind of flowered sheet you see on your parents' bed, is something that looks like it could be a hunched-over person. Josh smiles and gives me the thumbs-up sign. I feel a sudden explosion of heat on my face and turn away so Josh won't see it, but I end up staring straight at Marissa, who is leaning back in her chair, her legs crossed neatly so her hot pink mini-skirt won't ride up too high and break the dress code.

"Did you forget to rub in your blush this morning?" she whispers loudly, rubbing her cheek with her fingertips as if demonstrating what I need to do.

I throw down my backpack on my desk, grope for my notebook, and scribble the date at the top of the page just to avoid looking at Marissa. When all the kids are seated, Mr. Sampson says, "Well, today Josh is going to finally share his journal with us, along with a special guest." He gestures to the sheet-covered object and goes to the back of the classroom to give Josh the stage.

Josh hops onto Mr. Sampson's desk and sits comfortably with his legs apart, hands on his knees. He's wearing a faded blue t-shirt, which brings out the blue spot in his hazel eyes.

"Hey, what's under the sheet?" Marissa leans forward with her chin resting on her hands as if she's posing. The tips of her long blonde hair, which she must have dyed pink last night, brush the top of her desk.

"You'll find out." Josh flips open his journal as if he's eager to begin reading.

"But I want to know now," Marissa says in a pouty way that boys seem to find cute.

"Marissa, patience is a virtue," Mr. Sampson pipes up from the back of the room. "Speaking of which, I'm still waiting for your first journal entry." When Marissa's face turns the color of red licorice, I turn to her and rub my cheek with my fingertips and mouth the word, "Blush."

"Okay," Josh says, "I know you're all dying to hear what I've written in my journal." He dramatically clears his throat as he tosses back his head so his wavy brown hair flies off his adorable face.

"It's got to be about lacrosse," yells out Sam Neufield. He pretends to throw Josh a ball with an imaginary lacrosse stick.

"Sorry to disappoint," Josh says. "But I had other things on my mind at midnight when I finally started doing my homework." He grins that chipped-tooth smile and all the girls beam back as if he's smiling just at them. I'm no exception. I want to believe that today that smile is for me.

"I know, Mr. S. This journal-thing is way overdue. Sorry." Josh then starts reading a fictionalized conversation between himself and his great-grandfather, the doctor. He uses a really deep voice to play the great-grandfather, sitting with his back straight and his legs pressed together. When he plays himself as the little kid, he opens his eyes really wide and moves his arms and legs like a hyperactive kid. He's a really good actor. Everyone starts laughing when they realize what he's doing.

In a little-kid voice, Josh tells his great-grandfather about all the advances that have been made in medicine since his time, like heart-bypass surgery, organ transplants, and laser eye surgery. "And you wouldn't believe the cosmetic surgery, Great-gramps," he says, his voice squeaking. "They have television shows where they turn perfectly fine-looking people into creatures who look like mannequins. Pretty soon everyone on our planet will look like everyone else."

In a deep voice, Josh says, "I know how those perfect people must look. Just like your great-grandmother, Pearl. She was a fine-looking woman. Beautiful alabaster-white skin that never saw the sun." He touches his face lightly, and I swear he's looking at me. But then I think, "Get a grip, Allie. He would never like you over beautiful Crystal."

I stop my daydreaming when I hear Josh as the great-grandfather continue, "Oh, my Pearl was so nice and plump. She weighed about 160 pounds. All my pals thought I was lucky to be married to such a splendid woman." As the class laughs, Josh laughs along with them.

Josh, as his great-grandfather, tells us what it was like to be a small-town doctor during the Depression, when most people could only pay him with things like corn from their farm or firewood. But the part that really puts us on the edge of our seats is when he starts reading about what it was like to go to medical school. "We all had to buy our own cadavers to dissect. In case you don't know, a cadaver is a dead human body."

"Ew," shrieks half the class in unison.

"Pipe down," says Mr. Sampson. "It's not as if you haven't heard of death before."

"That's so weird that you could buy a body," Mathew Huddle shouts out. "Did they have a store for them or something?"

"No," Josh says, "Doctors bought them from places like funeral homes, where dead bodies of unknown people would be delivered. And you're about to meet one of them. Because, here's Charlie."

And with that, Josh rips the sheet off the object standing next to him, and there it is—a real skeleton of a man attached to a pole, a string tied to his skull making him stand up straight.

Some of the students yell out in surprise and there is laughing from several of the boys as Josh introduces the skeleton.

"Is that what happened to the cadaver your great-grandfather owned?" Mathew Huddle leans forward to get a better look.

"Yes. I'd say 'in the flesh' except there's none of that left," Josh says. "After the skin decomposed off the cadaver, doctors would keep the skeleton and sometimes they'd display it in their office."

"It's so yellow." Marissa looks like she's going to throw up.

"Well it's over a hundred years old. It's not going to be white like those fake Halloween skeletons. Does anyone know what this bone is?" Josh points to the thigh bone.

"I know! I know!" Mr. Sampson shouts, waving his hand wildly from the back of the class, in imitation of some of the more enthusiastic students like Mathew Huddle.

"Yes, Mr. S." Josh says, "although I'm tempted not to call on 'hyperactive hand-wavers.'" This is Mr. Sampson's expression.

"It's called a femur," Mr. Sampson says. "It's the largest bone in the human body."

"Very good. You get an 'A,' Mr. S." Josh says and everyone laughs. I wish I could be as comfortable as he is with teachers. I'm always piping up with the right answer to get teachers to like me. "There are 206 bones in the human body if anyone wants to come up and count."

Most of the kids gather around the skeleton except for a few who hang back. Marissa moves to the back of the room, opens a book, and pretends to read. But I can tell she's really scared of the bones. I force myself to go up and look at Charlie. I don't want to be a wimp. Plus I'm way too curious about what a real skeleton looks like.

I try to imagine Charlie before he was a skeleton. I wonder if he had kids. And how sad it was that he died all alone and didn't even have a funeral where people could have talked about what a great guy he was. Then I think about Dorothy May and how her bones are somewhere buried underneath the sand in Provincetown Harbor.

Sara Borden sits very close to the skeleton and draws in her sketchpad. Today she wears a headband made of paper clips. When I sneak a look over her shoulder, I see she has sketched the bones very realistically.

"So this is what we look like inside our skin," I say. "It looks like a bunch of dog bones strung together with string." Sara doesn't look up, just keeps drawing. She must still be mad at me for the other day, thinking I totally agree with what Marissa said about her. Like everyone else, Sara must think we're still best friends.

I decide to try again. "The only difference between this skeleton and mine is that mine will have chocolate permanently stuck to it because I eat so much of it."

Sara smiles hesitantly, but keeps her head down. Her hand moves rapidly as she continues to draw the skeleton. Yes, she still thinks I'm an idiot. But before I have time to worry about it, Josh comes up to me and whispers in my ear, "Whew, I did it."

"You were great," I say. "Maybe you should try out for the school play."

"You think so?" he asks.

"Definitely." I'm sure Marissa is giving me an evil look, but I don't care.

As we all crowd around the skeleton, Mr. Sampson places his hand on its skull and says, "'Alas, poor Yorick. I knew him well, Horatio.' All right, Shakespeare fans, which play is that quote from? I'll give you a hint. It's from the grave-digger scene."

"Come on, Allie," Josh says. "I'll bet you know." He nudges me lightly with his elbow. I can't believe he's being so nice to me.

"Maybe someone else wants the rubber chicken today." I know people must get sick of me always having the right answers. It's not my fault I have a good memory.

"What? Do you read Shakespeare instead of watch TV or something?" asks Mathew Huddle, thinking he's being really funny.

"Come on, Allie. What's the answer?" Mr. Sampson asks. "Don't let the Shakespeare-challenged mob frighten you away from learning to love the Bard."

"Okay. It's from *Hamlet*," I say. And as Mr. Sampson throws me the rubber chicken, I notice Josh smiling at me. Could it really be that he likes smart girls?

28

I practically skip down the hall to my next class. I wish I could throw my backpack up in the air and yell, *"Josh likes me!"* Someone has tapped me with a magic wand and turned me overnight from a girl with frizzy red hair into a beautiful princess with golden hair and tiny feet. Oh, this is going to be a great year. I can't wait to go on our field trip to Plimoth Plantation, so I can sit with Josh on the bus and lean into him when the bus makes sharp turns and then he'll put his arm around me to protect me from the bumps. Thank you, Mr. Sampson for suggesting I help Josh with his journal. Oh, I can't believe how lucky I am. I am the luckiest person in the universe. Nothing can go wr...

Smash! I run right into her. And actually knock her over, spilling her backpack all over the hallway.

"Ow!" she shrieks, and Suzanne comes running, her jet-black ponytail bouncing against her back.

"Crystal! Are you all right?" Suzanne pulls Crystal to her feet, smoothing down her tiny skirt, which got caught up in

143

the back, revealing her black thong. There are containers of eye shadow and lip-gloss everywhere. It looks like a department store make-up counter was knocked over.

"Did you see that?" Crystal screams. Her perfect features contort into a monster face. "That bulldozer just ran me over." All around her students scurry like elves whose only purpose is to take care of Crystal. They run up and hand her the contents of her backpack—books, papers, lip-gloss, and moisturizer.

"I think we got it all, Crystal," says one of the elf-students, presenting her with the last item—a pack of cigarettes. Crystal grabs it and tosses it down the hall. "That's not mine, you idiot!" she screams, even though everyone saw it fly out of her backpack.

The student mumbles, "Sorry," under his breath as he backs away. Crystal's other helpers follow his lead and sneak away down the hall into classrooms. One of the boys secretly picks up the cigarette pack and slips it into his pocket.

"What are you, on drugs or something?" Suzanne grabs my arm and holds onto it really tight. She has a new henna tattoo on her hand. It says, "BFF: SCM," which I assume stands for "Best Friends Forever: Suzanne, Crystal, and Marissa." I wonder if Marissa has one, too. She used to hate tattoos.

"Let me go. I have to go to math." I try to pull my arm away from Suzanne, but she holds on tighter. Crystal grabs my other arm. I thrash at them, but with two against one, it's no use. I can't break away.

"Conference time, Allie," Crystal says. "Step into my office."

My heart beats fast. I enter the girls' room; the bright fluorescent light shines right into my eyes. Crystal gives me a shove forward, and I slide across the icky lime-green tiles. "Stay away from Josh," she says.

"You know Crystal has been seeing him, so butt out." Suzanne nudges me into the sink counter.

"I'm not doing anything. He's in my class." My voice is shaky and I stare down at some crumpled paper towels on the floor to avoid looking at Crystal and Suzanne. "I didn't know Crystal was seeing him. I've never seen them together."

"What do you need? Pictures to prove it?" Suzanne asks, touching her earlobe where three holes are red and infected. I heard she had them done at a piercing party where the girls stuck needles through each other's earlobes.

"No," I mumble.

The bell rings and I try to ease myself away from the counter, but Suzanne blocks my way. "You're not going anywhere."

"I've got to get to math class." I turn and try to squeeze my way past her, but Crystal stands in front of me, glaring.

"I think it's all right if you miss a few minutes of 2+2, Nerd Brain." Crystal grabs a piece of my hair and slowly pulls it till it starts to hurt.

I have to think fast. I point to the mirror over the sink. "You know this is a two-way mirror with security guards on the other side."

Suzanne looks worried, then whispers something into Crystal's ear. Crystal shouts, "There are no security guards. She's lying."

Crystal moves towards me, but then gets distracted by her own reflection in the mirror and reaches into her backpack for a burgundy-colored lip pencil, which she uses to outline her lips. She stops for a moment as if she's just remembered I'm still there and turns her head slightly toward me. "Josh will never like you. You're too ugly," she sneers.

The word "ugly" hits me like a punch in the stomach. Suddenly it feels like there's no air in the girls' room. Who am I kidding? Maybe Josh really does think I'm ugly and is just being nice to me. I study Crystal's face next to mine in the mirror. With her blonde hair and tiny figure, she could be in a fashion magazine. There's a reason she's popular. Look at my hair. It's sticking out all over the place, and even though Crystal has just fallen on the floor and been humiliated, she looks totally put together. Why would Josh ever prefer me to her?

"And ugly girls never win," she continues as she fills in the outline with a dark red lipstick, smacking her lips together as if kissing herself. "So face it, you're nothing but a big loser."

Crystal starts writing the word 'loser' in big letters on the mirror with her lipstick. "Yeah, you're nothing but a 'L-O-Z-E-R.'"

How dare she call me a loser and act like I don't exist, while she stares at herself in the mirror putting on her lipstick? I grab Crystal's lipstick out of her hand.

How dare she burn my hair and trip me in the hall? I change the "Z" to an "S" on the mirror. "You spell it with an 'S,' you big loser!"

And worst of all, how dare she steal Marissa away from me and then tell me I can't be friends with Josh? I start to write, "CRYSTAL IS THE LOSER," as I say it out loud.

Crystal yells, "Get her!"

As Suzanne lunges towards me, I grasp onto a hunk of her long hair and tug really hard. I shriek when it pulls off her head and I'm left holding a long strand of black in my hands. That's when I realize it's a hair extension.

Suzanne yells, "Give it back!" And I instantly throw the hair at her like it's a snake.

"If she likes my lipstick so much, perhaps she'd like a makeover." Crystal squeezes my hand until I drop the lipstick. While Suzanne holds my arms behind my back, Crystal starts to draw lines on my face with her lipstick.

"Don't!" I yell as I wriggle one hand free. I ease it into the sink and turn on the water full blast. And yes, as I had hoped, in the mirror, I see the reflection of the person I have called forth with the water—Dorothy May.

"Thanks for coming," I say.

"Who are you talking to?" Crystal drops my arm for a second.

"Might these be the ladies who hurt thee?" Dorothy asks.

"Yes. And they're trying to hurt me again," I say.

"Stop being so creepy." Suzanne backs away.

"Look. All you have to do is say you won't talk to Josh and we'll leave you alone," Crystal says.

"Dost thou wish to cease conversing with a boy named Josh?" Dorothy May asks.

"No, I don't want to," I say.

"What do you mean you won't stop talking to Josh?" Crystal hisses. "You're just a little nothing." Her eyes blink rapidly. "You couldn't possibly think he'd ever like you over me."

"Dost thou have affection for this Josh?" Dorothy May asks.

"Yes, I kind of do," I answer.

"You think he likes you!" Crystal shrieks.

"Then fight for him." Dorothy May smiles sadly. *"I only wish that I had had the strength to do the same. I should not have given up in my quest for William's love."*

"But I'm not as pretty as she is." I stare intensely at the mirror, trying to pat down my frizzy hair.

"That's what we've been telling you," Crystal says. "That's why Josh likes me and not you. Right, Suzanne?"

"I don't care," Suzanne says. "This is getting beyond strange. She's not talking to you, Crystal. Look at her. She's talking to something in the mirror. Didn't Marissa say Allie talked to some ghost from the Mayflower?" She tugs Crystal's arm. "Come on. Let's get out of here."

"I believe the lady Crystal is afraid thou hast gained this Josh's affections," Dorothy May says.

"Maybe you're right," I say.

"I most certainly am," Dorothy May says.

"Of course I'm right," says Crystal. "Josh will never like you."

"Perchance this is a decision for Josh," Dorothy May says.

"Yeah. Why don't we let Josh decide? Maybe he doesn't like Barbie dolls with no brains." I start to walk toward the bathroom door, but Crystal grabs me and shoves me hard. I fly back into the sink, the hard edge smacking my spine.

"Ow!" I cry out.

"Baby," says Crystal. "That didn't even hurt."

"Methinks this trollop wears too much paint. Dost thou not think she requires a bath?"

"A bath?" I ask.

Dorothy May points to the sink. *"A dousing needs be in order. Much like was bestowed upon the witches in my day."*

As Crystal heads towards me, I turn on the cold water full blast, push my palm up against the faucet, and direct the strong stream of water against Crystal. Water gushes all over Crystal's perfect hairdo, and soaks her pink outfit so that it becomes transparent.

"Hurrah!" Dorothy May shouts as she claps her hands delightedly. I smile at the sight of a drenched Crystal.

Crystal screams so loudly I have to cover my ears because I'm afraid the decibel level will split my eardrums. And that's when the door bursts open and Mrs. Andreassi, the assistant principal, rushes in.

29

"Okay, who won Round One of the girls' room boxing match?" Mr. McGrath, the principal, asks as Crystal, Suzanne, and I sit silently in cold metal chairs facing him. Crystal has changed out of her wet clothes and is now wearing her lacrosse uniform because it's the only extra outfit she had at school. Her hair is still damp and doesn't look as blonde as usual. Suzanne nervously plays with the hair extension in her hand, wrapping a chunk of the fake dark hair around her finger. I tried to scrub the lipstick off my face, but there's still a red-brown stain that looks like blood.

Crystal glances at Suzanne as she pretends that she's rubbing her eye with her fingers. But I can tell she's trying to show Suzanne the henna tattoo on her hand that matches Suzanne's—probably to remind Suzanne of her loyalty to Crystal.

"Interesting tattoo, Crystal. Let me see." Mr. McGrath walks around his desk and takes her hand in his. He's an older man with thinning grey hair, thick glasses and a slight stoop. He's always been really nice to me because my mother works with him.

"Oh, and I see Suzanne has one too." He leans in extremely close and lifts up his glasses to read the tattoo on Crystal's hand. "'BFF: CSM.' Hmmn. I'd have to be an awfully out-of-touch middle-school principal if I didn't know 'BFF' means 'Best Friends Forever.' And I assume the other initials C and S stand for Crystal and Suzanne. But the M, now I don't suppose that stands for Allie."

"No," Crystal says with a pout, as if she shouldn't have to deal with someone as unimportant as the principal. "Can we go now? I'm supposed to be taking a make-up test in gym." She hides her hand in the pocket of her sweater so Mr. McGrath will stop talking about the tattoo.

"CSM isn't some kind of secret society, is it?" Mr. McGrath asks. "Because you know that's not allowed here." He leans up against the edge of his desk. "Or a gang. We don't like those much either."

"No, it's not a gang or a secret society. Just a group of friends," Crystal says in an exasperated way, flipping her hair with her hand. "We are allowed to have friends, aren't we?"

"Absolutely. Just as long as they don't lead to fist fights. Suzanne, do you have an opinion on this?" Mr. McGrath asks. "Or do you always let Crystal answer for you?"

"It's just a friendship tattoo. That's it." Suzanne bites her lips, looking as nervous as I feel. I've never been sent to the principal's office. And fighting in the bathroom is about the worst it can get. I just hope my mother doesn't...

But as soon as I think that, my mother rushes in, and throws her arms around me. "Allie, are you all right? Oh my God! What's on your face?" she cries out.

"I'm fine, Mom," I mumble, looking down at my shoes. "It's just lipstick."

"Lipstick? On your cheeks? Who did this to you?" She stares at Suzanne and Crystal.

"Hey, she's the jerk who threw water at me, ruining my..."

"That's enough, Crystal." Mr. McGrath cuts her off.

"Oh, like I'm really going to get a fair trial here." Crystal leaps up from her chair.

"Sit down, young lady." Mr. McGrath deepens his voice so it sounds scary.

Crystal sits down again, but protests, "It's not fair. Allie's mother is the school psychologist and she hates me."

"Oh, Crystal, you've met Mrs. Toth?" Mr. McGrath asks. "Was it a social occasion?"

"No." Crystal tightens her lips as if to prevent another word from flying out.

"Was she the one who got in trouble for taking a photo of a girl in the locker room and posting it on the web?" Mr. McGrath asks my mother, trying not to smile.

My mother doesn't answer, probably because this stuff is supposed to be private, while Crystal stares down at her nails, as if deciding when to schedule her next manicure.

"Were any of the girls hurt in the fight today?" my mother asks, clutching my shoulder. Mr. McGrath shakes his head, motioning for Mom to sit down in a comfortable leather chair next to his desk. She shifts from Mom mode to professional mode, smoothing down the skirt of her crisply-ironed suit, and automatically reaching into her pocketbook for a yellow writing pad, which she'll use to write up a report about our fight.

"The nurse has already checked out the girls for permanent damage. Just a couple of scratches, although there might be some bruises tomorrow." Mr. McGrath sits back in his seat. "I hope you can get to the bottom of this, because these three haven't been very forthcoming."

"I can try." My mother's voice sounds strained, which is understandable. I mean, how embarrassing is it for the school psychologist to have her kid get caught having a knock-down, drag-out in the girls' room. "I first want to apologize if my daughter was involved in any kind of fight, although in her defense, I do have to say that this is very unlike Allie."

"See, she's sticking up for Allie again. How come my mother's not allowed to be here?" Crystal asks in her snottiest voice.

"I tried calling your mother, but all I got was voice mail," Mr. McGrath says, "and in my phone list, there's a no-call policy next to your father's name."

"Mom's afraid he'll kidnap me," Crystal says proudly as if she's a big prize everyone is fighting over.

"So, can any of you girls tell me what the fight today was about?" my mother asks, her pencil poised over the yellow pad.

The room goes quiet. Crystal looks up at the clock, waiting for the bell to ring to end the school day. Suzanne imitates Crystal, although she chews on a couple of fingernails and her eyes blink rapidly as if she's holding back tears.

My mother looks at Crystal and Suzanne. Then she pushes her glasses up on her nose and stares straight at me. "Allie, I think it's time you told us what happened at the Teen Center last week."

"The Teen Center?" Mr. McGrath asks. "Was there a Teen Center incident I'm not aware of?" He stares at my mother, astonishment on his face.

"Allie?" my mother asks, but I shake my head no.

"All right, then I guess I'll have to speak."

"Mom, don't," I beg. I glance at Crystal. All the color is draining from her face.

"I'm really going to get in trouble if I miss that gym test, Mr. McGrath." Crystal stands up and pulls her pocketbook strap over her shoulder.

"Sit down, Crystal." Mr. McGrath slams his hand down on his desk. Crystal jumps and drops back into her seat. "I'm afraid this is a little more important than a couple of jumping jacks."

My mother's words come rushing out. "Something happened to Allie at the Teen Center. When she came home that night, her hair was burned." Instinctively I cover my hair with my hand. Mr. McGrath gets up from his desk, walks around me and lifts up the back of my hair. I sit up very straight and try not to breathe.

My mother keeps talking. "Allie cried all that night. But she won't talk about it. I think perhaps today's girls' room incident has something to do with what happened that night." After she's finished talking, my mother places the palms of her hands on her knees and takes a deep breath like she does when she's exercising to her yoga tapes.

Mr. McGrath lifts up his glasses and peers at my hair. "Did you see a doctor about your burned hair, Allie?"

"I'm fine. It didn't burn my scalp or anything." Right now it's my face that feels like it's burning up.

"I want to know who did this to my daughter. Crystal? Suzanne?" My mother stands up and faces them. "You know both of you have come to my office before for another case of bullying. I'm beginning to feel that maybe these incidents should be recorded on your permanent records."

"What?" Suzanne bursts out, fear in her eyes. "Don't colleges see that?"

"Don't listen to her. She's making it up," Crystal whispers to Suzanne.

"Mrs. Toth is telling the truth, And…" Mr. McGrath leans in and whispers in a conspiratorial way to Crystal. "I have to tell you, if this hair-burning incident, which I suspect you had something to do with, had happened on school property, you'd be kicked out of here so fast, you wouldn't even have time to clean out your locker." He crosses his arms and looks with narrowed eyes from Suzanne to Crystal and back again.

"My mother will kill me if she finds out!" Suzanne yowls. "She told me I'd be grounded for the rest of my life if I got in trouble again." She begins to cry. "I didn't do anything. I tried to help Allie."

"She did," I say, and stop when I see Crystal glaring at me.

"It's all Crystal's fault. She burned Allie's hair!" Suzanne cries out.

Crystal jumps up and screams at Suzanne. "You're lying. I didn't do anything to Allie! Somebody else must have done it, because we were in the Teen Center the whole time. Don't you remember?"

"No, we were in the woods and you threw a match at Allie's hair and called her 'Tick' because you didn't want her to hang around with us," Suzanne cries out. "All week I've been scared the cops were coming to my house. I'm not sharing the blame like you made me last time. This was your fault! Not mine!" Suzanne wipes her eyes with the bottom of her sweater. Her face is blotchy from crying and pools of black mascara collect under her eyes.

"Thank you, Suzanne," my mother says. "Can you tell me who else was there?"

I start to yell out, "Don't!" but it's too late.

"Marissa," Suzanne blurts out, followed by one long sob.

30

"I just wish you had told me. That's all," my mother says. "Why didn't you call me earlier to pick you up from the Teen Center?" I'm sitting across from her at the kitchen table eating the delicious apple Mom baked for me. The sweet smell of brown sugar reminds me of sledding in winter when she would have baked apples waiting for me when I got home—the only time I've seen Mom use the oven.

"I didn't want to get anyone in trouble." I scoop another mushy piece of Cortland apple in my mouth. It slithers down my throat, warming my body.

My mother frowns as she sips her coffee. "You mean Marissa."

"I know it was stupid considering she wasn't being very nice to me. I guess I thought if there was any chance, we'd be friends again..." I stop, realizing how stupid that must sound, like I'm so desperate to have her as a friend. Laszlo ambles over to me and puts his head in my lap. I pat him as he stares up at me with his big friendly eyes encircled by black patches.

"Maybe you and Marissa just outgrew your friendship," Mom says.

"Well, Marissa did anyway." I gulp down my milk.

"I'm very disappointed in Marissa," my mother says.

"Yeah, well, I guess I am, too." Mom reaches across the table and takes my hand in hers. It feels warm and safe so I don't try to pull it back. "You know, school psychologists are a little like fortune tellers. Maybe because we see the same things happen every year with a new crop of students. As kids get older, they usually find friends who have similar interests. I predict that eventually you would have tired of someone whose only obsession is learning to be a model."

"I've been friends with Marissa for so long, I don't think I can remember how to make new friends." The clock over the sink, which whistles a different bird song every hour, tweets six times like a chickadee. Can it really be six o'clock already? I guess one thing you can say about getting in a fight in the girls' room is that it makes the day go really fast.

My mother turns the palm of my hand over and pretends to read it. "I see a new friend in your future."

31

It's six o'clock in the morning when my yawning class members and I crawl onto the bus. Because it's a three-hour drive to Plimoth Plantation, the school has provided a more luxurious vehicle than a school bus. Well, at least it has a bathroom. I convinced my mother to pack me some good snacks for a change—only one healthy red apple, and the rest is delicious junk food. I know her generosity with high-fat-content potato chips won't last.

The seat next to Josh is taken by his shaggy-haired lacrosse buddy Sam Neufield, but Josh gives me his big chipped-tooth smile and a wave as I walk past him. Even though my daydream of leaning into him on the sharp turns is thwarted, I'm almost glad that I don't have to think up things to talk about this early in the morning.

Marissa is sitting in the back by herself, her bright pink sweater draped over her shoulders. She's spread her stuff all over both seats, making it obvious she doesn't want anyone to sit with her. Since Suzanne and Crystal aren't in our class, they're not on this field trip, and I guess Marissa doesn't think anyone else is cool enough to spend a three-hour bus ride with. I certainly won't bother trying to sit with her. This will just have to be the first field trip in seven years where we haven't sat together.

There's an empty seat next to Sara Borden. Today, her straight brown hair is pulled back tightly into a pony tail with a Chinese scarf tied around it and she's wearing earrings made from tiny paper fans that really open up.

I have butterflies in my stomach as I ask, "Do you mind if I sit here?" She hesitates. I wait for her to say no, but then she moves her backpack from the seat, and sticks it between her legs.

"Go ahead," she says, although she doesn't look at me.

As I settle into the seat, I blurt out, "I'm sorry."

"For what?" Sara asks.

"Oh, you know, the other day in class, when Marissa said...I didn't really feel the same way, but I was feeling weird and...I don't know. I think it's great you draw."

"I didn't think you appreciated art."

"I do."

"Well, then thanks. So you don't think I'm a Picasso wannabe?" she asks.

"No. Well, unless you wannabe."

Sara smiles.

"I hope you know I didn't think that about you," I say.

Sara nods and goes back to sketching with a charcoal pencil in the sketchbook in her lap.

"What are you drawing?" I ask.

"Just some Pilgrims like these." She opens a library book and shows me a photograph of people dressed as Pilgrims at Plimoth Plantation. "I like to keep track of what I do."

"Oh, it's like a diary in pictures," I say. Her drawing is really good. She could be a professional. The folds of the woman's dress are perfect. It looks just like Dorothy May's dress. "Do you find this stuff interesting?" I point to the Plimoth Plantation book.

"Sure," she says.

"Good, because I hope people aren't really bored today. I feel kind of responsible—you know, since I brought the story of a couple of Pilgrims to class."

She laughs. "Don't worry. I have even stranger ancestors than you."

"What do you mean?"

"I'm descended from Lizzie Borden."

I remember my mother telling me about this famous murderer. "No way! Like in that poem, *'Lizzie Borden took an axe, gave her father forty whacks?'*"

Sara smiles. "*'When she was done, she gave her mother forty-one.'* She killed her father and stepmother with an axe. You can't get much weirder than that. Here. Look." Sara flips through her sketchbook and shows me an illustration of a woman in old-fashioned clothes sitting quietly by a fire. "This is how I imagine Lizzie in her calmer days before she went crazy."

"It's hard to imagine what would drive someone to do that," I say.

"Sugar," she says. "She probably ate too many cupcakes that day."

"Yeah, or her anti-depressant prescription ran out," I say, starting to laugh, which feels really good since I haven't been laughing too much lately.

"Or her father told her to go chop down some wood, but Lizzie had lost her glasses and mistook her stepmother for a tree." Sara starts laughing, too.

"Or her father said to Lizzie, 'You ask too many darn questions. You must ask forty wacky questions a day.' And she thought he said, 'You must axe me forty whacks a day.'"

We get sillier and sillier and soon we're giggling so hard, I start to snort, and that makes Sara laugh even harder.

"Hey, quiet up there," Marissa yells out. "I'm trying to get some sleep."

"Quiet yourself!" Josh yells back. "They're just having a good time."

"Yeah," shouts Sam. "What do you want, Marissa? Someone to sing you lullabies?"

I sneak a peek at Marissa who looks shocked. She probably can't imagine someone sticking up for me over her. Especially someone as cute as Josh. I smile as I settle into my seat, happy to wallow—at least for a little while—in the feeling that maybe Josh likes me better than Marissa. When has that ever happened?

"Hey, do you mind if I sketch you?" Sara asks.

"Me?"

"Yeah, you have such cool hair. It'd be really fun to sketch."

"You're kidding? Right?" I hold out a red curl. "You can't even get a comb through this."

"Hey, celebrities pay a lot of money to get their hair looking like yours—with all those great curls." She starts sketching curlicues and ringlets. "Who would want boring straight hair if you could have hair like that?"

"Okay. If you say so." I pass my fingers through my hair and catch a glimpse of it in the bus window. It does look kind of pretty today, framing my face nicely.

As she continues sketching me, Mr. Sampson hops on board the bus. He's wearing a black Pilgrim hat pulled low over his buzz-cut. He's got on high-top basketball sneakers and a basketball jersey over a button-down shirt.

Mr. Sampson shouts, "Okay, Pilgrims, we're off on our voyage. Remember, your assignment is to come up with an account of our trip."

Sara calls out, "Hey, Mr. S., can it be in...?" She holds up her sketchbook.

"Absolutely, Sara," Mr. Sampson replies. "You can draw your assignment. You can also pair up if you like."

Sara turns to me. "How 'bout since you're an experienced journal writer, you do the writing, and I'll do the pictures?"

"Sounds perfect." I smile at Sara and she smiles back.

Just as the bus driver is about to shut the door, Mathew Huddle runs on, holding his glasses onto his face. Breathless, he says, "Sorry, I'm late. My mother made me eat a hot breakfast." He scrambles through the bus until he finds the only empty seat—the one next to Marissa. I have to laugh when I see her roll her eyes as she reluctantly removes her coat from the seat.

"Thanks, Marissa. It's almost worth being late because I get to sit next to you." Mathew flops down in the seat next to her.

Mr. Sampson counts heads to make sure everyone is here, then shouts out, "Last one to Plymouth Rock is a rotten egg!"

The bus starts up. I sit back, and for the first time in a long time, I relax.

32

Mathew Huddle yells out, "Hey, there's the Mayflower!" and those of us who have been sleeping on the bus, wake up to see the Mayflower II, the reproduction of the original Mayflower, docked in Plymouth Harbor.

We scramble off the bus and make our way toward the dock. Sara stays behind, sitting on a bench in the little park so she can sketch the Mayflower II from a distance. As I step onto the four-masted ship, Josh walks up to me. Once again, I'm struck by how tall he is. "I'll bet you never thought it would be so small," he says.

"Can you believe a hundred and two people lived on this boat for over two months? And that's not even including the sailors." I hope I don't sound too much like a teacher.

"Crammed together with nothing to do," he replies. "With no TV or video games. That's an awful lot of playing charades or whatever they did in those days." As if he's starting to play charades, Josh pulls on his ear and says, "Sounds like…"

"Torture." I finish his sentence. Josh laughs and his eyes crinkle warmly. A man with a bushy beard approaches us. He's dressed like a seventeenth-century sailor, wearing a billowy sailor's shirt and drawstring trousers.

"I do not know as I have heard of this 'charades,' but the twenty-eight children on board liked a game of marbles or cat's cradle to pass the time. Or mayhaps I would come upon them playing with the ship's cat and our two dogs." The sailor pulls on his beard as he talks. "'Course the harsh voyage sapped the strength of the poor little ones, and many's the time I would find them casting the contents of their stomachs overboard."

"Allie, let this be a lesson to you." Josh wags his finger as if scolding me. "If you ever get the chance to time travel and visit those Mayflower ancestors of yours, don't do it."

"I promise. Crowded on this tiny boat with the only food being rotten meat crawling with maggots is not my idea of fun," I say, grimacing.

"Meat?" The sailor rubs his stomach to show how hungry he is. "Dost thou know of someone who hast meat? I would not mind the maggots if I could lay my hands on some meat."

"Tell me where the snack bar is, and I'll get you a maggot-free hot dog." Josh winks at me.

"Hot dog?" The sailor looks shocked. "Even if I was to starve, I would not eat the meat of that loyal beast."

Josh and I laugh and, out of the corner of my eye, I catch Marissa staring at me. She's leaning against the ship's railing by herself and has this dazed expression on her face as if she's trying to wake up from a bad dream.

"Can you tell me where the forecastle is?" Josh asks the sailor. He pronounces it "fo'c'sle."

"Aye, thou wilt climb that ladder over yonder." The sailor points to a ladder leading up to a small deck.

"'Fo'c'sle?' Is that a word every guy knows?" I ask.

"It's a requirement for being a guy," Josh says. "Like ballpeen hammer."

"Ballpeen hammer?"

"Ask your father," he says. "I'm going to check out the forecastle. Save me a seat at lunch." He puts his hand lightly on my back, almost a little hug. Even after he heads for the ladder, I can feel the warmth from his hand.

I watch as Josh scoots up the ladder with his long legs and arms like an Olympic gymnast climbing a rope. I can't believe Josh told me to save him a seat at lunch. Of course, I won't be able to eat a thing.

"And what wilt thou be wishing to see, good mistress?" the sailor asks me.

"I'd like to see the place where the Pilgrims lived while they were on board. You know, where they ate and slept," I say.

"Aye, what we call the 'tween decks. That's where most passengers spent their time. Mighty crowded, it was. 'Tis below the main deck and above the hold where we store our cargo. Make your way down those stairs." The sailor points to some wooden steps. "Good day to you."

"Thanks." I head for the steps.

I pass by Marissa. Her arms are folded tightly across her chest as if she's cold. Well, no wonder. She's only wearing a thin sweater and a short skirt. Marissa yawns and says, "This is so incredibly boring."

"I don't think it's so bad." I try to get past her, but she steps closer to me, as if she wants to talk.

"That's because you were hanging around Josh." She gazes up at what I now know is the forecastle of the ship. I can see Josh's dark hair bobbing up and down as he chats with another sailor.

"What? Are you going to report back to Crystal—News flash: Allie was talking to Josh." I start to move away from her, but again, she moves closer.

"No. I don't care who you talk to. To tell you the truth, I don't think there was ever anything going on between Crystal and Josh." She stares off into the water, trying to avoid my eyes. I guess she's a little embarrassed about it, since they all made such a big deal out of the supposed Josh-Crystal connection.

"Really?"

"Yeah. I think she liked him, but it never went anywhere."

"Great. So she tries to beat me up over nothing." I don't mention the embarrassing trip to the principal's office that I also had to endure.

"Yeah, I heard about that thing in the girls' room. Crystal can be very possessive."

I can't believe I'm wasting my time talking about the horrible Crystal even when I'm hundreds of miles from home. I decide to ask Marissa something I think needs to be answered. "Marissa, do you really like her?"

Marissa hesitates for a moment, then says, "Sure. She's my friend."

"And it doesn't bother you that she's probably the meanest girl on the planet?" I blurt out.

Marissa seems to shrink, hunching her shoulders forward and grabbing her arms tighter around herself. "She's not that bad. She's even done some nice things for me like, you know, she gave me a makeover." She rubs the heavy eye shadow on her eyelid with her finger. "And she didn't charge me or anything."

"How nice of her. And I'll bet she doesn't even charge you for being her friend." I start to turn away.

"You don't understand," Marissa says. "She's really good at doing makeovers. She wants to be a make-up artist—you know for movies and stuff. So some girls pay her to give them makeovers 'cause she's so good."

"Okay. Whatever you say."

"Allie, can I ask you something?" She looks down at the wooden deck.

Here it comes I think. Marissa wants to be friends with me again. She's finally realized what losers Crystal and Suzanne are. But what will I say? Do I still want her as a friend after all that's happened?

"Would you... Would you want to do the project with me?"

"What?"

"The project Mr. Sampson is making us do for this field trip. You already know all this Pilgrim stuff from your mother. It'll be a breeze for you."

I start to laugh.

"What's so funny?"

I shake my head. "Here I was worrying about whether you were going to ask me if we could be friends again." I throw back my head and laugh really loudly. "And all you want is for me to do your homework for you."

"That's not what I meant."

"Sure, Marissa. Sorry. But I already have partner for the project."

"Who? Josh?"

"No, Sara Borden."

Marissa wrinkles up her forehead. "But she's such a weirdo. She never says anything, just draws in that notebook all the time. It's creepy."

"I like her. She's nice. And she's interesting," I say, and start to turn away.

"But you hardly even know her," Marissa says.

"After spending a couple of hours with her on the bus, I think I know her pretty well." I look her straight in the eyes. "And obviously a lot better than I know you anymore."

I march past Marissa towards the narrow wooden stairs. In all our years of friendship, I was never the one to walk away first when we had an argument. I put my foot on the first step.

"Allie," she calls. "Allie."

I stop there, one foot going down, one foot not moving. For months I have dreamed about this moment. Where we could erase everything and start over again, just the two of us. But the amazing thing is I don't want to. I'm not sad about not being friends with Marissa anymore. After all, I've had the last word and I'm finally free of her. I move my feet down the steps.

33

As I make my way downstairs to the 'tween decks, the first thing I notice is how cramped and dark it is. The ceiling is very low and the only light filters in from tiny slatted openings. I kneel down on the wooden deck and look through one of the openings. I can barely make out the ocean water right below me.

"You have chosen the spot where at night I lay my head upon a thin mattress of straw." Dorothy May crouches down next to me.

"I did? This very spot?" I ask. "How weird."

"Aye, thou must have been drawn to it." Dorothy May has changed out of the velvet gown I gave her, and is once again wearing her Pilgrim clothes.

"You didn't like my dress?" I ask.

"'Twas beautiful," she says. *"But I discovered that I am most comfortable in mine own clothing."* Dorothy takes me by the hand and leads me to a wooden chest. She makes a place for me to sit beside her.

"'Tis time for me to go home," she says softly.

"Home? But where is home?" My voice cracks.

"Here."

"On the Mayflower? But it's so depressing."

"Not so de-pressing. I thank thee for bringing me to this place. I quite like this new Mayflower. Mayhaps because everyone on it nowadays has bathed."

"Doesn't this bring back bad memories of what happened to you on this ship in 1620? Why would you want to stay here?"

"'Tis the only place my son would know to find me." She folds her hands in her lap and looks steadily into my eyes.

"Oh," I say quietly. "After you find him, maybe you could still come visit me."

"Nay," she says. *"My journey with thee has ended. I will miss thee."*

I look away, blinking back tears. I can't believe Dorothy May isn't going to be in my life anymore. I thought she'd always be around. I think about trying to convince her to come back with me, but when I turn to her, I see that her eyes are dark with sadness.

"Well," I say, "I hope you find your son."

"'Twould help me rest easy," she says. *"I most desire to tell my son how sorry I was to have left him behind."*

"You know, he probably won't look the same." I don't want Dorothy to be too disappointed even if her son does come. After all, when she last saw him, he was three years old.

"Aye, as thou hast informed me, he was fifty-eight years when he departed this world. I have lost his boyhood. No matter. 'Tis his spirit I most desire to make the acquaintance of."

Although Dorothy speaks boldly, as she glances around the ship, she looks afraid. I take her hand to try to calm her fears.

"What if he dost not forgive me for leaving him behind?" Her lips tremble.

"He has to know all the suffering you've been through. I don't think he would put you through any more."

"Dost thou think that is true?"

"I do. Besides if he's your son, he has to have your heart. And it's a pretty big one." I put my arms around her. "Thank you, Dorothy. You were my friend when no one else would be."

"'Twas my pleasure," she says. *"I am most honored to call thee my friend."*

My throat tightens and a tear rolls down my face. "I'll miss you."

"Thou wilt not have time to miss me now that thou hast made new friends." She points towards the staircase as Sara calls down the steps.

"Come on, Allie," Sara says. "It's lunchtime. Josh and Sam are saving us a table."

"In a minute." I turn to Dorothy May. "Are you sure you'll be all right here?"

"Aye, I am prepared to wait an eternity for him if need be."

"I hope it doesn't take that long." I wrap my arms around Dorothy again and give her a big hug. "Good-bye, Dorothy." I wipe my eyes, turn around and leave her, slowly walking up the steps. When I reach the main deck, I see Sara adding a last-minute detail to her sketch of the Mayflower.

"Great drawing," I say. "We can use it for the cover of our project."

"Good idea." Sara closes her sketchpad. "Have you thought about what you want to write about?"

I take one last look down the stairs. Dorothy May is sitting on the wooden chest, staring straight ahead with her back ramrod straight. She looks so lonely that I want to run back down and make her come with me, but just as I step toward her, something shimmers into view. Suddenly, there he is, standing before Dorothy—a man with curly grey hair, wearing a black Pilgrim hat, dark breeches, and a white ruffled shirt. Dorothy May cries out. She jumps up and throws her arms around him.

"Oh, wonders!" she cries out. *"Thou art here!"*

"That's so great! Her son has come for her!" I say as a shiver runs through my body.

"What?" Sara asks.

"Nothing. I just got an idea of what I can write about."

"Good." Sara grabs my arm. "Let's go. I'm starving."

"Me too," I say. And as Sara and I walk to the Mayflower Diner together, we never stop talking. It's like we've known each other forever.

THE END

Author's Note

I f you're like me, you want to know what is true in a novel.

Dorothy May was definitely a real person who came over on the Mayflower with her husband, William Bradford. But whether she jumped off the ship, as my book states, or accidentally fell to her death is disputed, as there were no eyewitness accounts.*

My mother—a romantic at heart and the family historian—told me that Dorothy May had jumped overboard, heartsick and lonely. Poor Dorothy May despaired on that

---

* In the eighteenth century, a Puritan historian named Cotton Mather recorded that Dorothy May accidentally fell off the Mayflower. But a modern historian, Nathaniel Philbrick, wrote in his book, *Mayflower: A Story of Courage, Community, and War*: "That she fell from a moored ship caused some to wonder whether she committed suicide. Dorothy certainly had ample reason to despair: She had not seen her son in more than four months; her husband had left the day before on his third dangerous trip away from her in as many weeks." (With a small group of men, Dorothy May's husband had left the Mayflower to search for a place for the Pilgrims to settle.)

—PHILBRICK, NATHANIEL. *MAYFLOWER: A STORY OF COURAGE, COMMUNITY, AND WAR*. NEW YORK: VIKING PENGUIN, 2006, P. 76.

cold night in 1620 for two reasons—she desperately missed the son she'd been forced to leave behind in Holland, and she suspected that her husband, William Bradford, was still in love with Alice Carpenter.

In Holland, before William Bradford had met Dorothy May, he proposed marriage to Alice Carpenter, but Alice's father had forbidden it, as he didn't foresee a prosperous future for his daughter with young William, an orphan and a weaver by trade.

After Dorothy May died, William discovered that Alice was now a widow, and he sent a letter asking her to join him in America. In 1623 on a ship called the Anne, Alice came to Plymouth and married William, who was by now the governor of the Plymouth colony. (A governor! So much for Alice's father's prediction.)

Unlike Allie in my story, I am not descended from William and Alice, but rather from one of Alice's sons from her first marriage. Eventually, these two sons joined her in America, as did Dorothy May's son. They all grew up together in Plymouth with Alice and William, along with the three children they had together.

So, Dorothy May was a real person. That she would want to know that her son was all right is speculation, though one I'd like to think is true.

I was happy to give her the chance, as the ghost in Allie's pool, to find out.

About The Author

Sari Bodi's short stories and essays have appeared in publications in the United States and England, and her comedy sketches on BBC Radio. Her plays have been performed off-Broadway and by high school students around the country. In New Haven, Connecticut, Ms. Bodi served as the literary manager for the Long Wharf Theatre and taught playwriting in a magnet high school specializing in the arts. She lives in Westport, Connecticut with her husband, their two children, and their dog, Eolas, who as a young pup came over from Ireland, thus continuing the family tradition of immigrating to America. For more information or to contact Sari, visit her website at *www.saribodi.com*.

Ribbons of the Sun: A Novel
By Harriet Hamilton

In my village we grow flowers. Big, strong, beautiful flowers. Carnations, roses, calla lilies, daisies—all kinds of flowers. When their buds start to open and they are the most beautiful, we take them to Santa María del Sol and sell them in the marketplace. My mother always told me I was her special flower, a gift from la Virgen. That's why she named me Rosa.

Twelve-year-old Rosa begs to go with her father to the city to sell flowers, and when that day finally comes, she can barely contain her excitement.

But her joy turns to despair when she realizes the real reason for her trip to the city—her impoverished family has been forced to sell her into service as a maid.

Assaulted and humiliated by the *patron*, she is thrown out on the hostile city streets to fend for herself. Alone and without hope, her beliefs shattered, Rosa learns to survive and triumph in this emotionally violent but deeply spiritual coming of age story.

A story that will linger in your mind for years.

"the life story of an Indian girl on the threshold of adulthood, cast out by her own people to work in a household that rejects the culture from which she came...an unflinching view of the antagonisms among racially divided groups, yet it conveys the strength of a people who retain their roots."

June Nash, social anthropologist,
author of *Mayan Visions: The Quest for
Autonomy in an Age of Globalization*

"Hamilton depicts Rosa's indomitable spirit as she eventually reaches into the depths of her spiritual background to recognize her own self-worth. While the story of child exploitation has been told before in other novels, the narrative's simplicity and lack of graphic sexual detail make the book an excellent choice for YA as well as adult fiction collections."

Library Journal, Sept. 15, 2006

ISBN: 978-09768126-2-3   176 pages $8.95   14 to adult

Brown Barn Books
www.brownbarnbooks.com

The Separated: The First Tale of Terre
by Troon Harrison

Each solstice, summer and winter, Vita must weave the magic spells that protect the mythical corno d'oro, the great creature with the golden horn who keeps the world in balance. Tempted by the lure of the city and the huge white castle where the evil Lord Maldici gives glorious balls for the nobili, she chafes under the responsibility she bears.

Giovanni, Vita's childhood friend, dreads his destiny as a pirate, forced to prey on merchant ships for gold—battling, killing, stealing, devoting his life to acquiring gold and jewels.

Marina tries vainly to weave the spells her outcast sea-witch mother forces her to learn, but she longs to escape the sea to live on land—as a healer and gardener. But can she escape her powerful mother and the bounty of the sea?

This glowing tapestry of a violent Italian Renaissance land brings to life three compelling young people, exotic creatures, sorcery, meadows of wildflowers, scheming sorcerers, magical battles, cruelty, desire and love.

"A skillfully crafted novel of fantasy action/adventure, *The Separated* is very highly recommended for its creative and magical world and tangible vivid descriptions of battles of faith and revolution."

Midwest Book Review, June, 2006.

ISBN: 978-09768126-1-6 $12.95   12 up

Brown Barn Books
www.brownbarnbooks.com